"Say Something, Please,"

she whispered. All of a sudden her eyes were filling up. . . .

Her tears moved him to response. "I didn't mean to upset you, Kate. I'm such a fool! I knew if I ever touched you again this would happen. Please forgive me. Sweet Kate, don't cry."

She was no longer in danger of tears, but she willingly let him kiss her lids and her hot cheeks, marveling at the exquisite gentleness possible in such a big, powerful man. She would have trusted him with her life right then; she trusted his strength, his sensitivity. . . . He couldn't possibly belong to the same sex as Andrew—not even to the same species.

LYNNETTE MORLAND
lives in New York and considers it the most glorious city in the universe (although she plans to give London a chance to snatch the title). She loves antique clothing, drinking espresso in Greenwich Village cafés, reading in bed, and staying up all night to write her books.

Dear Reader:

I'd like to take this opportunity to thank you for all your support and encouragement of Silhouette Romances.

Many of you write in regularly, telling us what you like best about Silhouette, which authors are your favorites. This is a tremendous help to us as we strive to publish the best contemporary romances possible.

All the romances from Silhouette Books are for you, so enjoy this book and the many stories to come.

Karen Solem
Editor-in-Chief
Silhouette Books

LYNNETTE MORLAND
Occupational Hazard

Silhouette *Romance*

Published by Silhouette Books New York

America's Publisher of Contemporary Romance

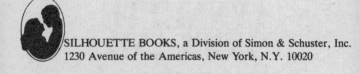
SILHOUETTE BOOKS, a Division of Simon & Schuster, Inc.
1230 Avenue of the Americas, New York, N.Y. 10020

Distributed by Pocket Books

ISBN: 0-671-57339-X

First Silhouette Books printing January, 1985

10 9 8 7 6 5 4 3 2 1

Map by Ray Lundgren

To "B" for his inspiration and generosity

Occupational Hazard

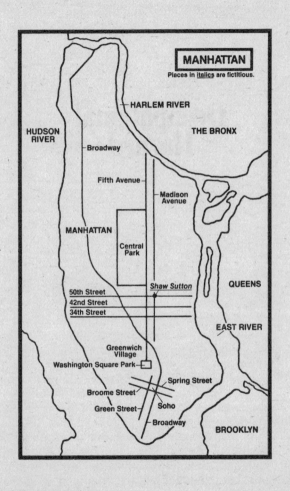

MANHATTAN

Places in _italics_ are fictitious.

HARLEM RIVER

HUDSON RIVER

THE BRONX

Broadway

Fifth Avenue

Madison Avenue

MANHATTAN

Central Park

QUEENS

Shaw Sutton

50th Street
42nd Street
34th Street

EAST RIVER

Greenwich Village

Washington Square Park

Spring Street

Broome Street

Green Street

Soho

Broadway

BROOKLYN

Chapter One

Although it was a weeknight, Weeds shook from its floor to high gilt ceiling with dancing. On the big movie screen in front of the stage videos played, and the sound system roared out beat-heavy music. Kate Angel sidestepped a couple swinging each other in reckless loops and wished she had brought a friend or two with her. She could have mentioned it to Ben. Weeds was not quite his tweedy grad-school style, but he had asked her out so many times unsuccessfully he might have come anyway. She didn't like dancing with any random male who grabbed her arm, and she felt uncomfortable hanging out at the bar talking to Terence. The club was understaffed that night, and he had to run like a racehorse up and down the bar pouring drinks and passing them to the hands that sprouted from the crush of people. The music was so loud that when he threw a remark her way she had to read his lips—not her strongest talent. She became tired and irritated at having to shout "What?" all the time.

She looked at her watch—a quarter to twelve. Pop Quiz ought to be on stage by midnight. Allowing for a forty-five-minute set and a few minutes spent backstage congratulating them, she ought to be home shortly after one. It wouldn't cut into her sleep much, and she would have been properly social. Esme had warned Kate that she must try being social once in a while. The further up in the art world she moved the more necessary it would become.

Kate realized that fate had been with her this time. Pop Quiz *could* have played their first important gig a week earlier, when she was in the midst of preparing her own show. Exhausted from the final frantic days of framing drawings and arguing over the lighting at the gallery, she would have shown up at Weeds a total zombie. And the next day, even more short of sleep, she probably would have committed some exceptional piece of stupidity—like hanging a painting upside down. It had certainly been done—though not by her. But this time everything had worked out. Frank and Sully had moved her canvases to the Ridley Gallery on schedule. The electricians had finished rigging the lights on schedule. Pete had given her the walls she wanted with no argument whatsoever. The printer had even finished the invitations in time for her to address and send them to her friends for the opening. She was now a woman of leisure, until the next major project fell on her.

The guys in the band had been sweet to invite her. They probably felt, rightly, that they had paid her an embarrassingly small sum for the painting they used as the cover of their new single record. True, she could have gotten much more through the gallery, but she remembered vividly how it felt to be a struggling young artist. She held on to that feeling with grim purpose—it kept her art very tense and fresh.

The tonic water was weak with melted ice, so she squeezed up to the bar rail to snare Terence's attention. He seemed to have been looking for her—he leaned across the spiral piles of cocktail napkins and shouted into her ear, "Would you take over for a minute?"

"What?"

"Take over for me. The manager's got a problem up at the ticket window. I'll be right back." Before she could protest, he had flipped open the swinging panel and dragged her in.

"What do I do if someone asks for something weird?"

"Pretend you didn't hear them. That's what I do. And the baseball bat is under the sink."

Baseball bat! Fine, Kate thought grimly, prepared for a riot to begin at any minute. She was disappointed on this count. After a few awkward moments spent locating the beer refrigerators, she was uncapping and pouring with the best of them and scraping her tips into a plastic cup for Terence, even though he was a rat for sticking her here. No one seemed to pay attention to her, though—less than when she was a lone female on the floor. It was pleasant to be able to examine her patrons without having to worry that they'd mistake her aesthetic interest for something warmer. Perhaps she could turn part of the scene into a painting. She liked the rich colors of the bottles lined up behind her, the liquid reflections from the beads of moisture on the polished wood. She liked the angles at which the dancers squeezed themselves forward to get a drink. They made such an intricate, writhing pattern of colors and textures—spangled gold, black-and-white-checked plastic, loud yellow-and-blue houndstooth, stark red, fine black wool.

Fine black wool? Her consciousness realized that this was out of place. She followed the spotless sleeve up to a broad shoulder, a dazzling collar of white silk, and then to the tanned face of a quietly smiling man, vividly handsome. Her safe behind-the-bar persona dropped away and she was suddenly very conscious of a part of herself she had suppressed for years: Kate the woman, Kate in a severe black linen dress with black and white bangles on her wrists, huge white earrings banging against her bare neck, her hair pulled into a knot high on her head from which it fell like a cascade of black silk. This man's dark eyes made her remember these things and wonder about their effect. He was taller and so much more self-possessed than the kids who bopped around him. That, even more than his business suit and his strong good looks, made him stand out. A redheaded boy in a black leather vest craned around him and whined unattractively, "Come on, Grandpa! Order or get out of the way. I need a beer, man!"

Kate felt offended for the quiet man. Grandpa indeed! He couldn't be more than 39 or 40, and he had an aura of health and vitality about him that made everyone else look positively ill. She walked over to him very deliberately, quelling the juvenile with a look, and smiled. "Yes?"

He beckoned to her to lean across to him and then spoke directly into her ear. "May I have a Chivas on the rocks, a wine spritzer, and a beer for the young man?" His voice was deep and relaxed, obviously not often used for shouting in rock clubs. She felt a tingle race through her skin from his nearness, as if he had actually tickled the wisps of hair around her ear. She summoned all her own grace to set the drinks before him, sure her hands would choose that moment to drop the bottle of scotch. They did not. He graciously presented the beer to the redhead, who grimaced suspiciously but took it. Then he placed a twenty-dollar bill into Kate's hand, took up his glasses, and maneuvered skillfully back into the crowd without waiting for his change. She watched him intently, unable to shake off the warm feeling he had inspired. His dark wavy hair showed above the crowd, and she tracked him to the stairway that led up to the reserved tables on the balcony. A woman waited for him. Of course. And, of course, she was languidly beautiful, her blond hair swept into a perfect French twist, her bronzed skin glowing against a dress of the precise yellow that made Kate herself look jaundiced. He must be a record-company executive, she decided—the table upstairs, the corporate look, the sleek companion. Definitely out of her world—and why would she want him? She had sworn off wanting men, particularly ambitious men, although she still enjoyed their occasional company.

These reflections absorbed her until she felt her arm being shaken. Terence had returned. "Wake up! Somebody hit you over the head? Your band's going on."

She barely had time to ring up the three drinks and stuff the change into Terence's tip cup before Pop Quiz crashed out onto the stage.

Later, head ringing from the pulsating guitar rhythms and the extremely loud vocals, Kate es-

caped from the dance floor. Backstage the crowd
was smaller, if just as frenzied. The members of Pop
Quiz must have invited everyone they knew to the
club that night. That suited Kate; she would be able
to sneak away shortly and not be missed.

It turned out to be less easy than she had hoped.
The drummer snared her from the throng of well-
wishers and dragged her to a corner where a small
party had gotten going. The band members were so
pleased with their performance, they could barely
contain themselves. Plans for their future worldwide
blitz and eternal fame shot through the air like
bullets, and Kate had to add a little enthusiasm
before they would release her.

When she finally convinced them that even artists
must get their rest, her head was ringing from the
music *and* the vodka she had drunk. She rarely
drank hard liquor, and this reminded her of why.
Putting her hand out to the rough wall to guide
herself through the dimness, she started looking for
the stairway and got lost. Really, this was ridiculous!
She wasn't *that* tipsy, and Weeds wasn't that big, but
she had absolutely no idea where to go. The music
downstairs was so loud the walls reverberated evenly
on every side.

"Damn!" she muttered.

"May I be of some help?"

The voice was vaguely familiar. She turned and
saw the handsome dark-haired man. He had his
hands thrust deep into his trouser pockets, flaring
the jacket back away from his spotless shirt and
revealing a lean, hard-muscled torso. He put the
frantically dancing kids downstairs to shame. She
hoped her eyes weren't totally round; she feared she
had been staring at him rather noticeably.

He came forward a step, moving easily with the

grace of a cat. That's what he reminded her of—a big, dangerous black panther—except for the good nature evident in the smiling mouth and sparkling dark eyes. "Or should I just go away and leave you to whatever makes such a beautiful woman look so angry?"

"No!" she said quickly, flushing. Had that sentence come from any other man she would have thought it slick and insincere. But she felt he really meant it. He thought she was beautiful! Well! This whole night might just have been worthwhile.

His smile deepened, exposing white teeth. "No—which? Can I help or should I go?"

"Maybe you can help. I've misplaced the exit."

He looked mildly surprised. "You haven't worked here long, then?"

"Worked here . . . ? Oh!" Of course—he thought she was a bartender downstairs. "No, I . . . this is the only night . . . I came up here to congratulate the band . . . oh, it doesn't matter." She shut up, sure the long, rambling story of why she was roaming around lost was more than he would want to hear.

"All right." He chuckled. "I think I can extricate you from this labyrinth—I brought a ball of string with me and tied one end to the main doors."

"Who's your Ariadne?"

"Pardon me?"

"Ariadne gave Theseus the ball of string when he went into the labyrinth to do battle with the Minotaur."

"My, my—a classically educated bartender! I'll have to come here more often. I guess I haven't got an Ariadne." He removed one hand from his pocket and pressed it lightly behind her elbow. The barely perceptible touch seared through her like electricity.

Why was she reacting so strongly? He was beautiful and charming, but there was something else about him that pleased her more—an innate graciousness, an easy, unspoken strength. She thought he'd make a good Greek hero, even if he was so dark.

"Are you a record-company executive?" The question popped out before she realized how he might take it. A club like this would be filled with hopeful musicians looking for contact with a record company.

"No. I'm in advertising."

Her heart sank. Advertising, what else? Pick the one profession she considered more awful than any other and it would be advertising. She had good reason, after all. . . .

He saw her disappointment. "Sorry. Why? Are you an aspiring musician?"

"No—a painter. I just asked out of curiosity. I wondered why you were here."

"Maybe I'm the father of one of these kids."

"No!" she protested, shocked.

He laughed at her look of horror. "You're right, I'm not. Ah, here we are—the mouth of the labyrinth."

"Thank you."

"My pleasure." He bowed slightly, and the old-fashioned gesture charmed her. Then he was gone. Her elbow felt inexplicably cold as she walked out through the doors.

The man in the black suit stood just inside the door of Weeds caught in an attitude of indecision. It was an unnatural state for him and, after an uncomfortable moment, he was amused at himself. At *his* age, with *his* history, he had been seized by an insane desire to charge out into the street after that wonderful . . . well, "bartender" would have to serve, although it had become apparent that she must be something else entirely. However she had come to be there, she had plucked the evening out of an annoying, noisy string of such evenings spent in clubs and made it glow as brightly as those ridiculous plastic earrings of hers. He enjoyed a momentary vision of the things competing in vain with her delicately white skin. She had blushed when he offered his help upstairs. He didn't know any women with the modesty to blush; his own fault, no doubt. Why did he continue to go out with women like perfectly coiffed, blond Cynthia, now waiting for him in the VIP lounge; women who would have thought Ariadne was a new perfume or a Greek couturier? Did he just enjoy punishing himself? They were lovely, but this bartender had been lovely too—all dramatic contrasts of black and white, humor and suspicion, intelligence and that innate innocence that a very few select women kept no matter what happened to them. She attracted him in a way his chosen companions did not—therein lay her danger. Age and history had to have made him a bit wiser—he did not intend to make any more disastrous mistakes. He turned and walked deliberately toward the VIP lounge and Cynthia.

Esme's urgent call at ten the next morning woke Kate out of an uncomfortable sleep into the cool, sunny light of an early autumn day. A breeze sweeping through her floor-to-ceiling windows billowed the white gauze curtains she had hung from tracks to make partitions in the big loft.

"Wake up, kid," Esme ordered in her drill sergeant's voice. "You've got two hours to become a rational, articulate person and meet me for lunch."

"What's up? Why can't you talk to me over the phone?"

"Because when you're half asleep you're sure to say no to anything. 'No, go away, don't bother me.'"

"I'm inclined to say that now because you're being so darn coy."

"Tut tut, Katy Angel. Where's that new, forthright business woman you swore you'd be?"

"She's in the wardrobe with my clothes. I only put her on after I've had coffee."

"Then brew a pot quick! Meet me at Sunny's on Third Avenue at 37th Street. Noon."

"I'll bring my six-shooter."

Despite the quip, Kate woke very slowly. The crisp cotton sheets and the fluffy white comforter she had put on the big bed the night before felt glorious against her naked skin. The air's chill tingled the arm that had stolen out to hold the phone. She wanted to sneak it back under the covers and doze off for a few more minutes.

In a rush she threw off the bedclothes and jumped out into the elements. Her blood tinged her fair skin pink, trying to warm it. She hopped from one woolly rug to the next until she reached her old cedar wardrobe and snatched out a pale blue kimono.

Shivering less, she padded toward the kitchen, catching a glimpse of herself in the full-length standing mirror. She stopped and examined herself critically, remembering the compliment from the handsome man at Weeds and trying to see herself with his eyes. She wasn't sure she'd go as far as "beautiful," but she'd admit to "nice-looking." She was medium height, but so well proportioned that she gave the impression of being tall. Her figure was nice, she thought, though rather too generous for some of the boyish styles Esme could wear. She often bought dresses from the 1950s because she loved the nipped-in waists and full skirts.

She had a smooth, oval face, most notable for its large, violet blue eyes that peeked out from beneath thick black bangs. The ends of her eyes tipped up slightly, giving her an exotic look, and were heavily fringed with black lashes. The nose was short and straight, perhaps a bit too turned up for elegance; the mouth was full, the cheeks high and wide to complement the eyes.

As an artist she liked her hair best—it was thick and perfectly black, and she had learned to sweep it into an endless variety of styles. She usually wore it in a long, straight braid as thick as her wrist.

She didn't kid herself that she was the world's greatest beauty—for a long while, in fact, she had suspected that she must be unattractive and totally undesirable. Andrew had done that to her—the jerk. But over the years she had come to feel better about herself, and she realized that fine autumn morning that she quite liked herself again. That man at Weeds had awakened her to this splendid awareness. So an advertising man had proved useful for *something*. . . .

Her hair had freed itself in the night, as usual. She suspected that she slept like a dervish; her feather pillows always turned up across the room, and sometimes she woke up with bruises on her arms—perhaps from flinging them against the massive wooden headboard.

Her studio was somewhat neater than usual, since she had finished preparing for the show. The easels stood as bare as winter trees, and the paint-encrusted tarps were folded against the walls in dark mounds. Even the ever-present smells of turpentine and dammar varnish had faded to a point where the aroma of a pot of strong coffee could overpower them.

Coffee was exactly what she needed—mugs and mugs of it. Her kitchen opened off the main space, next to a skylighted bath. Those two modernized rooms were the only concession Kate had made to domestic life. Her painting needed much more energy and attention; she was willing to let normal life squeeze in around the edges of her art.

She took her coffee to the low rope chair near a tall window. That chair, another made of canvas and tubing, and several creamy Moroccan cotton pillows made up her living room. Her friends were all limber enough to sit six inches off the floor, although Ben had threatened to buy her a real chair. He said her arrangement reminded him too depressingly of his poor undergraduate days. She wondered why he hadn't adopted a more prosperous look now that he was a professor at New York University. Instead he affected the slightly threadbare carelessness of a distracted intellectual, like his many friends involved in unending years of graduate work. He liked to associate himself with The Humanities and The Arts and other grand ideas in capital letters. Kate sometimes wondered whether he had latched onto her because she was a painter and could add to his menagerie of colorful acquaintances. Certainly he hadn't enrolled in her evening class in drawing at New York Art and Design through any overpowering desire to learn to draw—but rather to enjoy the atmosphere of Art. Then she decided she was being too critical of the poor boy. He was handsome and pleasant and he just liked to sit in normal furniture.

The thought crossed her mind, unbidden, that the dark-haired man from the club could probably make himself at home on a floor cushion. He looked as if he'd be at ease anywhere. Why had she thought of *him?* Time to get another painting launched if her mind was turning to men. . . .

Her window looked down five stories onto Greene Street, a quiet, dark block between Spring and Broome Streets that was slowly being converted from grim industrial buildings to posh residential lofts. A couple of years before, she couldn't have afforded a stair landing in Soho, let alone her spacious loft. But, after everyone had advised her to get a normal job, move back to eastern Connecticut, or live with roommates in Brooklyn, dedication to her work had finally paid off. She sold steadily through the Ridley Gallery, took commissions, and taught an occasional drawing class at New York Art. No matter what she had been a couple of years before—penniless, emotionally ravaged, sick to death of painting—she had her life in order now. No one would wreck it again.

The coffee and the fall chill woke her finally. She left the mug in the sink and went to dress, planning to walk up to 37th Street. A hike of two or three miles would charge up her appetite and, since Esme might put their lunch on her expense account at the ad agency, Kate intended to have a very good appetite. She slipped into black tights and a voluminous red smock dress that came nearly to her knees. She belted it with a black rope, dug her black suede ankle boots from the bottom of the wardrobe, and added a necklace made from a black velvet ribbon and a little white cameo. Her hair, which tended to enjoy the breeze more exuberantly than other people's hair, she braided down her back. She strapped a suede pouch to her belt in place of a pocketbook. Years of lugging a heavy portfolio made her seek freedom from carrying pocketbooks whenever possible.

Esme was already in the restaurant, seated at a window table and sipping mineral water. She wore a gray custom-designed dress with a dropped waist, and she had bracelets of huge fake stones armoring her wrists. Her incredibly bleached-out hair stood straight up, except for two little pin curls in front of her ears. She looked even less like a corporate art director than usual.

Kate bounced in, invigorated by the walk and ravenous. "Hi! Thank God the bread's here." She split open a pumpernickel roll and buttered it before the waiter could even pull out her seat.

"I hate you," Esme informed her companionably. "I eat a buttered roll and I turn *into* a buttered roll."

"It's your Madison Avenue lifestyle, chicklet—taxicabs, heavy lunches with clients. The only exercise you get is picking up your magic markers from the stockroom." She snagged the waiter and ordered French onion soup, stir-fried vegetables over fettucini, and white wine. "Do you suppose their frozen yogurt is better with granola or walnut topping?"

Esme raised an eyebrow. "Talk about heavy lunches with clients!"

"I'm an artist—we're supposed to be eccentric, remember?"

"You're supposed to be starving," Esme observed drily. "Well, I must say you look in fine fettle."

"My fettle has never been finer, thank you."

"Then you won't mind my telling you that Keene Angel has just won a T-Square Award for overall excellence among small graphic arts studios . . . oops!"

The extent to which Kate minded showed in her suddenly grayed-out eyes and the sullen look that closed over her bright face like a cloud. Esme might be her closest friend in New York, and after Andrew's betrayal she had taken Kate by the shoulders and said with utter conviction, "No man deserves this kind of power over you, Kate." Esme had an unconquerable strength that Kate envied. After two years, mention of Andrew didn't exactly hurt, but it did cast a certain dimness over Kate's day.

"Sorry, Kate. But I *did* mean to shock you."

"Why?"

"Because you're becoming such a little fine-art princess."

"What?"

"Oh, how can I say it. . . . Look, this gallery stuff is okay, but it's not you. It's as if you've buried half your personality. When you were an illustrator you were doing work that meant something to you—you were communicating with people, touching millions of them with your sense of style and beauty. Remember how you used to say that if you could improve, by a fraction of a percent, the environment of the people who saw your paintings in a magazine or on a billboard, you would feel you had really done something?"

"That was a lot of pseudophilosophical garbage. I just liked being well paid by ad agencies."

"Cynic." Esme sneered. "You're not exactly a pauper now, you know. Peter told me you sold that enormous canvas of the stone wall to the Scovilles—the *banking* Scovilles. How much did you get for it?"

"Twelve thousand," Kate muttered self-consciously.

"Uh-huh. And where is the painting now? Their Upper East Side penthouse?"

"Actually, the colors harmonized better with the library of their house in Hyannisport."

"Where it will be seen by a couple of dozen

bluebloods who sail in for the spring regatta. What a glorious fate for a work of art."

"Esme, you're just prejudiced."

"Of course. I like what I do. You like what I do too."

Suddenly Kate laughed, breaking the tension. "You really know how to get me riled up, Esme."

"What are friends for?" The art director smiled with her big, crooked teeth, brown eyes lightening from their normally serious cast. "But really, Kate, *you* should be the one getting these awards. You would be if . . . if . . ."

"If Andrew hadn't changed the lock on the studio door and installed that redheaded little graphics student at my drawing table?"

"No, if you had recovered from that and gone on to form another company. You know you loved advertising and graphics—you got to work thirty hours a day at your painting and no one complained that you were antisocial, they said you were diligent. In its heyday Keene Angel was good for you."

Kate shrugged and stared morosely at her bread crusts. "It was a dumb company, and a dumb name too."

"The name sells work. So Andrew left a bad taste in your mouth for advertising. . . . One doesn't have to be a jerk to be successful, you know."

"You couldn't prove it by me."

"Thanks a lot. Am *I* horrible? Or am I a failure?"

"You're an exception."

"So's my boss."

"Huh?"

"My boss—you know, the man who runs the agency, the man who signs my paychecks?"

"Yeah, yeah. What does your boss have to do with me?"

"A lot," Esme murmured tantalizingly. "Maybe."

"A dark flicker of foreboding flashes through my mind." Kate frowned. "This is what you were afraid I'd say no to, right?"

"Right, but you're not going to say no—not if you're rational, as I asked you to be, and hear me out."

Kate laid her soup spoon aside and leaned back, arms folded. "I'm listening."

Esme propped her chin on her long-nailed hands and gazed at Kate appraisingly.

"Esme, I'm listening and you're not saying anything."

The blonde smiled slyly. "I'm psyching you out. The approach is critical. . . . Hmm, let's see. . . . I'll tell you about my boss first."

"You've already told me—he's really young to be president of Shaw Sutton and he's going after glamorous clients, right?"

"So you *have* been listening all these months! Go on."

"He does twenty times the work of any other exec—gets his hands dirty writing copy, correcting illustrations, directing photo shoots."

"What else?"

"What else? That's as much as friendship requires me to remember. To hear you talk, he's an advertising army—and the image is *so* appealing."

"Go ahead, be snide. The man *is* appealing. You remember Exquisites' Amber Soap?"

A prickle of interest started along Kate's spine. "Yes; they used to have those boring ads about the purity of their ingredients and how you could see your skin pores through their soap bars. Yuck!"

Esme's smile broadened. "I see you keep up with the trade."

"Well, maybe a little—but the new campaign is really striking. I mean, they went from a big yawn to all those gorgeous Egyptian-style ads about ancient amber jewelry and how it's supposed to protect you from evil and all that. Very stylish."

"My boss *is* very stylish. That's all his work."

"Hmm. So he's talented." Kate tried to appear unimpressed but couldn't quite manage it.

"Come on, Kate. I know that sort of stuff fascinates you. Admit it."

"Okay, okay. So your boss can resurrect the dead, and that's pretty neat. What does it have to do with me?"

"Well, Exquisites gave us that dud account as a test. Now they're dangling the prospect of a really big account if they like my boss's proposal. I'm one of the few people who knows about it because I'm going to be the art director for phase one."

"Congratulations! That news is worth a lunch out. I'm very pleased for you."

"That's *not* what this lunch is about."

"No?"

"No. I'm art director, but my boss already knows what illustrator he wants."

"Yeah?"

"You."

"Me! Excuse me while I choke to death on my olive. How does he even know my work?"

"Because I have that painting of yours in my office. He came in and saw it and said, 'That's the style I want for the Exquisites account.' I'm not kidding."

"And you said, 'Hey, sure, I can get that artist for you.'"

"No," Esme countered sarcastically. "I said, 'Oh, Jess, she can't possibly do this work for you—she's still emotionally wrung out because her lover ran out on her two years ago and left her with nothing but brains and talent.' Of course I said I could get you."

"You'd condemn me to painting portraits of bath-salts boxes?"

"You've done stranger things. Remember your series of paintings of antique silverware?"

"They were beautiful objects—all those reflections and swirls."

"Then you can't turn your nose up at jewelry. Yep, Exquisites is going to give us its top jewelry line—all those fantastic designers like Felice Champollion, Ivana Schiel, La Catelli. . . . My very mouth waters. The concept, and don't you tell a soul, is to do big portraits of the showcase pieces. They can be used as the main visuals in the print ads and can even be blown up into enormous backdrops for models wearing the jewelry."

"And I could approach them the way I do my other paintings?"

"That's the idea. . . . Ah, I can see the fire of enthusiasm in your eyes."

Kate tried to glow a little less obviously. She still had many reservations. "I won't have to sit in on meetings?"

"I'll do that and transmit the results to you."

"No unqualified morons making big black X's over my stuff?"

"Only qualified morons."

"No tight deadlines or corporate politics?"

"Now, Kate, be realistic."

"Hmm . . . I guess you're right." The silence lengthened as Kate's imagination played with the prospect of big, bold canvases of flashing jewelry. Through a haze of delight, she caught Esme's smug look. It brought her back to a more cynical reality. "I've fallen into your trap, haven't I?"

"Yep."

"So when do I go talk to your wonder boy? What's his name—Jess?"

"Jess Schuyler. You have an appointment with him tomorrow at two-thirty. Don't bother bringing your portfolio; he knows what your work is like—he just wants to meet *you*."

Chapter Two

The next day Kate navigated the spotless gray halls of Shaw Sutton with grave misgivings. Despite the cheery, busy look of the secretaries, she sensed the towering weight of a corporation poised over her head, waiting to drop.

When she was shown through one last set of silver doors, she stopped in surprise—the entire decor had changed from cold high-tech to an office with the woodsy warmth of an English country house. Books lined the walls, interspersed with framed awards and little art objects. Her feet sank into a nutty brown carpet. A few chairs and a love seat of walnut and russet tweed were grouped casually around a low table that held art and science magazines. A matronly woman smiled up from her handsome wooden desk—the word-processing terminal under her fingers was the only discordant note in the cozy atmosphere. She even had a brass bowl of daisies next to her telephone.

"May I help you, dear?" she asked, dropping her cat's eye glasses onto her chest, where they hung by a black cord.

"I'm Kate Angel. I have an appointment with Mr. Schuyler at two-thirty."

"Yes, of course. His meeting is running a bit late. Please take a seat. Can I get you some coffee?"

"No, thank you." Kate did not need caffeine; she had begun to feel uncharacteristically nervous as it was. Corporate slickness she could handle, however uncomfortable it made her. This hominess threw her off. It didn't jibe with her image of hotshot ad executives. At the sight of the middle-aged, unglamorous secretary, she had felt her estimate of this Schuyler go up another notch. The president of a big agency could have had his choice of beautiful secretaries, but he had this one. Interesting . . .

Kate sat gingerly on a soft chair, crossed her legs, and let her eyes seem to glance over the magazines. She couldn't have read if her life hung in the balance. The secretary checked to see that she had settled herself, then returned to her work. Kate struggled not to fidget.

Within a very few minutes, before her control could suffer a serious crack, Kate heard the low rumble of male voices from behind the large wooden door next to the desk. The secretary looked up at her and said, "That'll be the end of the meeting, hon."

The door opened and a confusion of suited, middle-aged men strolled out, filling the air with the smell of tobacco and, Kate could swear, Scotch. Great White Executives, she called them scornfully, feeling an unbridgeable distance between their corporate world and her very different one. She searched through the pot bellies and balding heads for some hint of which one might be Jess Schuyler . . . and stopped breathing. The man from Weeds! That quiet, gracious manner could not be mistaken, nor his exceptional looks. He was as tall as she remembered—six feet, maybe more—trim enough to wear sleekly tailored shirts, and carried himself with the fluid grace of a jungle predator— except that his claws were now covered in velvet. The men around him joked gruffly and clearly deferred to him.

"Well, Schuyler, it went exactly as you said it would. Where'd you get your inside information?"

He chuckled, a warm, throaty sound. "No secrets, Len, just good, solid research. You can thank Thelma here for the television ratings." He gestured generously toward the secretary.

"Still, it was a masterful piece of work," another man said. "Sure you're tied up this afternoon? I'd stand you to a Scotch."

"Send me a bottle, Mack—you made enough of a dent in mine at lunch."

There was general, untidy laughter. Jess Schuyler's eyes swept the room and fixed on Kate. What eyes he had—dark as coffee, sparked by intelligence and humor. She felt an indescribable thrill run through her. She sat unmoving on the couch as a smile slowly creased his cheeks. "I'm sorry to cut this short, gentlemen, but, as you see, I have a young lady waiting."

His colleagues noticed Kate for the first time. "Well, no wonder. I'd pass on a Scotch with a bunch of old war dogs too, if I were you," one of them said.

"I'll give you a buzz after I call Detroit, Jess."

The herd of business suits left with the collective grace of buffalo. Kate stood up, needing the slight advantage of height. Jess Schuyler's eyes flowed over her as limpidly as water, drenching her with their regard. She could hardly complain; she had examined him with the same scrupulous interest.

"Miss Angel?" he inquired in a voice so soft she wondered whether she had only imagined it. Following his gesture, she walked into his office. He murmured something low to Thelma and came after her, closing the door. Then he remarked thoughtfully, "Well, if it isn't the bartender!"

Her voice came out more acid than she intended, certainly more so than he deserved—his utter charm was affecting her adversely. "I was helping a friend last night. I am *not* a bartender."

"I was a bartender," he offered pleasantly. "That's how I put myself through college."

She thought he must be laughing at her and flushed. If he noticed he gave no sign, choosing to turn on a silk-shaded brass floor lamp that illuminated a deep-cushioned couch. "Please sit down and we'll talk."

She decided to lay her suspicions aside for a moment and took an end seat. He sat in a chair at right angles to her, smiling in that irresistibly easy manner she had begun to associate with him. No wonder he had all those big-timers enthralled. Charming men, dear God! The devil had created charming men to tangle her life into witch's knots. She braced herself.

"Can you handle pressure?" he asked abruptly, his mobile face falling into grave business lines.

"What?"

"To be ready for the Christmas season I have a magazine deadline in six weeks. That's a week of printing and preparing the ad mechanicals, complete with type and illustration, and a week and a half to get your paintings blown up into backdrops. That leaves just under four weeks for you to produce three large paintings of rather intricate pieces of jewelry. Commercial illustrators are used to deadlines. Fine artists are accustomed to pleasing themselves. Your work is beautiful, but I don't know how long it takes you. I don't want either of us to go into this with false expectations." His brown eyes drilled into hers, frank and uncompromising. She was glad she had been sitting down when he began his monologue; the force of his confidence and honesty beat against her like a storm. She should have been prepared for it—successful businessmen *were* aggressive. The gallery world had softened her. . . .

But not completely. The tough core she had retained, the determination that propelled her through life, tensed and made her lungs swell with the breath to answer him. "For your information, Mr. Schuyler, fine artists do not just loll about some patron's salon drinking champagne and occasionally flicking a brush at their canvases for effect. I work day and night at my art by choice. I just finished a series of eight oils and twenty-seven watercolors and matted and framed them myself for a show that opens at the Ridley Gallery in Soho in a few days. I have fulfilled commissions that would make your ad campaign look like a hobby. I've never missed a deadline, I've never turned in sloppy work, and I've never had my reliability questioned."

"Whew!" he exclaimed, smiling in genuine respect. "Remind me never to take that tack with you again."

"I *will*."

"I believe you. I wish my board of directors were so blunt—I'd like to know as clearly where I stand with them."

"Were they the men who just left?"

"Some. Plus a consultant and one of the corporation's lawyers. We're acquiring a couple of small companies—a graphics studio and a type shop. We met today to settle the last few details. Actually, I have to do a lot of hand-holding whenever Shaw Sutton makes a financial commitment like this."

"You have them eating out of your hand, I think."

"Until I make a mistake," he observed, one dark eyebrow lifting wryly. "I try very hard not to make mistakes."

His reference to the lecture she had undergone was clear. She valued honesty, but she never expected to find it so determinedly nurtured in the person of this ad man. Surprise threw her off stride. "Okay, go ahead with your third degree. I'll try not to jump down your throat."

He gave her a nod that seemed almost a salute. "All right, we've established that you *can* do this job. Why do you *want* to?"

"We haven't established that I *do*," she said coolly. Kate knew herself. She knew what tantalized her, what could overthrow all her hard-won habits of caution, and this man could. She had never eradicated the part of herself that flashed with excitement over the fast-paced, high-risk world of advertising. She liked working on a project that represented hundreds of thousands of dollars and many people's hopes and jobs. She throve on work and responsibility; pressure brought out inspiration from the deepest wells of her being. Nothing had been quite challenging enough for her since she had left Keene Angel. And here was a challenge facing her—a dual challenge, in fact: this man's painting job and the man himself. If she jumped in and made the commitment, she wouldn't be able to extricate herself regardless of what dreadful problems she discovered later on. Better to discover them right now.

Jess Schuyler was running his hand thoughtfully through his thick hair. She caught a glimpse of a gold cuff link nestled against his white silk shirt cuff. Its design was simple but impeccably elegant, and it emphasized the beauty of the warm, heavy metal. Like the man, she thought extraneously. He was made of some weighty, precious substance and cut in clean, graceful lines. What she saw before her was the real man, not a distracting illusion of suave manners.

The insight flared in her mind and was gone, leaving behind a little nodule of trust surrounded by a lot of confusion. What had she been looking at? A cuff link? A cuff link had decided her? I'm losing my mind, she thought in amazement. As caution settled once more on her, Schuyler continued.

"All right. I'll accept that your coming to talk to me means nothing." He smiled. "I won't hold you to anything you say in answer to my next question, but just pretend you want this job— Why do you want it?"

He was irresistible: The cockeyed grin that was reflected twinkled right up into his lively eyes, the way he sat next to her—so relaxed, yet tense with power. "I want it," she answered, "because more people would see my paintings in your ads than would walk through the Ridley Gallery in two thousand years."

His eyes flared in wonder. A giggle bubbled through her soundlessly. So she had thrown *him* off stride now—it was only fair.

"Is that ego, Miss Angel?"

"Perhaps. Or just an artist's very great desire to reach people. Whichever it is, I think you need it for your job."

"I do indeed," he commented, appraising her with new intensity. She met his eyes as frankly and coolly as possible, afraid her nerves must be showing through every pore. Being examined by him was different from being looked over by some jerk on the street, or even by a date. His regard was so . . . penetrating. She felt uncomfortably sure that he could see right into her heart and, if allowed to probe, could flush out all her secrets—her resentments and hurts, her needs . . . She stiffened and, to hide it, crossed her arms protectively across her chest.

"Pete warned me that you spoke your mind." He chuckled.

"Pete?"

"Pete Ridley—the owner of your gallery. Actually, the words he used were more on the order of 'Her tongue can singe the beard off your face.'" Schuyler rubbed a hand over his clean-shaven jaw. "I figured I was immune. Guess not. Look, we've been dancing around the most crucial factor in this decision—the jewelry. You can't know whether you want to paint it until you see it. Come with me." He rose to his full, black-suited height so abruptly Kate gasped at the transition. One moment he had been a charming inquisitor at eye level, the next he was a physical power, frightening in his speed and agility. She felt as if she had glimpsed the animal that propelled the man, and it was a bit more than she had expected.

She stared up with unconsciously widened eyes, feeling her heart slowly recover from the lurch it had given. Schuyler waited a fraction of a second for her to rise, then put his hand down. She took it without thinking and let him pull her smoothly out of her seat. She had to step forward to counteract the force of his aid, and she ended up much too close to him—close enough to smell a woodsy scent drifting from his tawny skin and to feel a vibrance in the air around him. She tugged tentatively at her hand and he released it, his fine eyes flickering with some unreadable expression.

"The jewelry?" she prompted, relieved that her voice, at least, remained steady.

"Yes," he agreed, his voice deep. He turned fluidly and strode through the quiet room. He stopped before a door she hadn't noticed earlier, opened it, and stepped through. Curious, though not eager to lose her protective distance, she followed, pausing at the threshold. Why, the office was a suite—he had a private room adjoining this one! A large, soft chair sat invitingly in the shadows against the wall, a book draped open over its arm. What looked like stereo equipment had been set into the dark, burnished walnut paneling.

He had just slid one rectangular patch of paneling over another and looked up from twirling a steel knob mounted behind it. "Come on in," he urged lightly.

As soon as she stepped through the doorway she could see recesses that had been hidden before. They held a huge bed made up in fitted cinnamon brown quilts that made it look like two squishy cushions in a pile. Folded neatly across the foot was a log-cabin quilt in terra cotta and white. The bed looked deliciously soft and scandalous. Did he spend a lot of nights here? And why?

"I keep the jewelry in this safe," he explained conversationally, working the combination lock. "It's not incredibly valuable, but the designs are still being kept under wraps. Ah."

Inside the safe she saw long velvet cases of a dusty rose color, stamped in silver with Exquisites' logo. Schuyler drew out a case, opened it, and showed the contents to Kate.

"Oh! How lovely!" She barely checked the impulse to pick up the choker revealed to her.

He caught her movement and said with a smile, "Go ahead, try it on."

She picked up the heavy, jointed piece of gold inlaid with ebony and white shell and held it up to her neck. He touched her arm lightly, directing her to a wood-framed mirror on the wall. The catch was strange, not immediately understandable. He allowed her a few seconds of fumbling and then draped the necklace around her neck himself and fastened it. She wasn't sure which pleased her more, the lovely jumble of colors nestled around her throat or the touch of his hands on the soft skin at her nape.

His voice was low and frankly admiring. "I haven't seen this worn before. It suits you well."

The mild compliment warmed her. Then all at once she realized how close she had gotten to feeling a sexual attraction for this man. Oh Lord, Kate, she groaned to herself. Pick a bum on the street, a juvenile delinquent, a certified lunatic—but not a man you might work for, and not an ad man! The internal warning strengthened her wonderfully. She was able to coolly slip off the choker, pour its liquid length into his hand, and stalk back to the safe outer office.

When Schuyler, wearing a puzzled and forbidding frown, followed her out, she was standing decisively in the center of the room. He walked to his desk, the frown pressing down his dark, straight brows. Kate could tell he didn't know what to make of her. She often didn't know what to make of herself.

He slipped his hands into his trouser pockets, revealing more clearly his slender hips and taut waist. Kate wished he were a bit paunchier, a bit inelegant, or more married. Heck, maybe he *was* married. Her mind jumped back to the blonde who had been with him at the club.

"Why were you at Weeds last night?"

This took him aback, but he answered, "I'm looking for a club to use in a commercial for a soft-drink company—they want to broaden their product's image from being a kiddie beverage to being a mixer for young, exciting adults. Your friend Esme will be handling the art direction."

"Did you find any young, exciting adults at Weeds?"

"One or two." His tanned cheeks crinkled with a grin. "I can supply my own young adults though—I needed a *place* with excitement."

He could probably supply his own excitement too, she judged privately, fighting against a nervous fidget. Well, that explained Weeds but not the woman. She didn't have enough nerve to ask him whether he was married. She wasn't sure she wanted to know, and it certainly wasn't the most natural question to pop out with during her own interview.

"You want to paint the jewelry, don't you." It was a statement rather than a question.

She blinked, knowing the time of decision-making had arrived. Was she ready to plunge back into this loved and hated world—with the enigmatic added element of Jess Schuyler? What did "ready" mean, for goodness sake? If she waited until the hurt and anger faded to nothing she'd wait forever. They were a part of her now; they shaped her reaction to things, cast their colors over her life in subtle and blatant ways. It was time to let other factors guide her. Suddenly she felt her frustration at the thought of undertaking another portrait, another teaching job, another year of sweating out paintings that would be bought by strangers and taken from her life forever.

Was it so bad that she was being offered a thrilling job by this magnetic, exciting man? Hadn't she better take charge of her recalcitrant emotions?

"Yes," she answered surely. "I want to paint the jewelry. I'll start tomorrow morning."

That night Kate sat in her rope chair, sipping white wine and staring moodily at the street scene beneath her window. She had been tricked. Not deceitfully tricked, but her own tangled feelings had been used to marvelous effect by Jess Schuyler. Oh, he was shrewd! Knowing nothing of her past, he had understood from her artwork and whatever Pete and Esme might have let slip exactly what would snare her interest—the importance of the campaign and that beautiful jewelry. So now she was hooked, excited by the job and terrified by the prospect of seeing Jess Schuyler every day.

The next morning Esme conducted Kate on a quick tour of the places at Shaw Sutton she'd be using: the art department, the cafeteria, the tool shop, and the stock room. Then Esme showed Kate the studio that would be hers. It was a beautiful studio, if blandly decorated. An entire wall of windows faced out over Manhattan from 50th Street north. To the upper left she could make out the spire of Riverside Church and the hazy gossamer of the George Washington Bridge. Closer and lower lay the brilliant, delicious reds and golds of Central Park in its full autumn glory. All the fancy apartment buildings ringing it made a white filigree of stone. Even Queens looked good.

"So, do you have enough space?" Esme planted her hands on her black-suede-covered hips and tried to look arch.

"Unless you want me to re-do the murals in Rockefeller Center—yes, I think this may just suffice. I've arranged for some of my own supplies to be delivered later this morning. Is there a freight elevator?" She kept her expression carefully casual.

"No problem. I'll tell the door guards. Look, I've got to run and make a couple of phone calls before our ten o'clock meeting. Will you be able to find your way to the conference room all right?"

"Meeting! You promised no meetings!"

"I lied. Well, can you find your way?"

"If I must. Really, Esme, I don't think I'll trust you any more. Okay, stop dancing from foot to foot. I can see you're in a hurry."

Indeed, Esme must have been in a hurry, or she would surely have questioned Kate about her "supplies."

With a glance at her watch, Kate decided to spend the twenty minutes before the infernal Exquisites meeting in planning where to place her plants and her stereo. It would also serve to take her mind off how eager she was to see Jess Schuyler again.

Esme introduced her to the account group in the conference room. None of them made much of an impression on Kate. The women were tensely composed and efficient-looking, uniformly disguised in skirt suits with moderately frilly blouses. The men, all in forgettable suits, greeted each other, and even their female colleagues, with a bluff, awkward comraderie that Kate found offensive. If one more person gave her a variation of "Call me Ed—we're all friends here," she thought she would point out specifically why they were not, in fact, friends at all and never would be. They reminded her of Ben's bearded, pipe-smoking friends who, utterly lacking British accents, went around jauntily calling each other "old fellow." A warning look from Esme made her bite her lip.

Then Jess Schuyler arrived. He wore a brown wool and linen suit with a shiver of mauve through the weave. His shirt picked up the brown, his tie the mauve. He surveyed the expectant group as he settled into the head swivel chair and then gave Kate a mischievous wink. What was it for? she wondered.

They discussed marketing concepts and consumer profiles and quality exposure—at least everyone did but Kate. She doodled on a pad and let her mind wander down somewhat embarrassing paths. Many times she found herself staring fixedly at Jess Schuyler's expressive face and comparing him to the other men. He had such an air of unaffected masculinity about him. The others had to force out throaty laughs and wriggled inside their clothes as if they were caged. Not Jess—he acted as if the world had been created just this way to fascinate and challenge him. So she stared unconsciously and filled her pad with little profiles of his straight nose and ever so slightly cleft chin. Once or twice he met her eyes. His look was even; it communicated nothing in particular, but it set her cheeks on fire. She noticed that it seemed to do the same to the other women in the room except Esme, who as a matter of policy never let men know what she thought of them. Kate wondered how many of these women Jess had shown into his nifty little office bedroom. Then she told herself to straighten up. She had even begun to think of him as "Jess."

She had been paying so little attention that the end of the meeting came unexpectedly. People rustled papers and laughed, muttering to each other things they had been keeping silent through the meeting. A diffident young secretary stuck her head around the door and said, "Jess, is there a Miss Angel here?"

Kate stood up and identified herself.

"There are two men bringing boxes into your studio, and they want to know where you want everything set." She looked extremely dubious about the message she was relaying; her eyes kept sliding to Jess for his reaction. In fact, a part of everyone's attention was on him. Kate understood that she had ruffled the smooth waters of Shaw Sutton. Esme laughed outright, but Jess said nothing, merely raising one eyebrow and letting a faintly quizzical smile tug at his mouth.

"Thank you," Kate said. "I'll go see to my things. If you'll all excuse me . . ."

She had reached the door when she heard Jess say, "I think we've covered everything, people. We'll talk again when we're farther along." She hadn't gone five feet down the hallway before he fell into step beside her. She gave him a small, noncommittal smile; she wouldn't offer any explanations until she had to.

"Did you find the meeting informative?" he asked blandly.

"No. I don't see why I had to sit through it, actually. You and Esme have already established the look of the campaign. If it changes you'll just have to get another artist."

"I wanted you to meet the people who are writing the copy that will be printed over your paintings, and those who will be selling the ads. And I wanted them to meet you."

"Fair enough."

"I also wanted you to feel a part of the team effort, as it were."

She stopped so fast she nearly knocked herself off balance. "Don't give me any of that ad lingo, Jess Schuyler! I worked in advertising for three years quite successfully."

He failed to respond satisfactorily to her indignation. He just cracked another delighted smile. "Did you, now? You'll have to tell me about it."

"No, I won't." She recovered some of her humor. "I'll have to take the Fifth Amendment on my late career in advertising."

"Very incriminating, is it?"

"Sordid," she agreed. Up ahead she saw Frank and Sully sitting on crates of her stuff outside the studio and dragging on cigarettes. She saw a scattered trail of leaves from her plants dribbling off down the hall. The two men had hauled her paintings to galleries many times and greeted her familiarly.

"Hey, Michelangelo, we set the easels and the plants in the sun and the stereo out of it, but where do you want this other stuff?"

"Hi, guys. Sully, Frank—this is Jess Schuyler, my boss."

Jess reached out his hand immediately, unconcerned about the grime on theirs. Frank sneered good-naturedly. "Your boss, huh? That's a good one. Nice to meet you."

Sully tried to look solemn. "My sympathies, sir." Kate glared at him.

She directed the unpacking quickly. Jess leaned against the doorframe watching, hands in pockets and an amused expression on his face. She kept feeling his eyes on the back of her neck.

Frank and Sully dusted off their hands on their pants, gathered up their dollies and hand trucks, and bade her good-bye. Their equipment made wheel tracks in the thick gray carpet. Jess stood aside as they left. She waited tensely next to a feathered palm. She felt that perhaps she had overdone this gesture of making the studio uniquely hers. Now he would say something.

He took his hands from his pockets, gave her a

long, level look, said, "Let me know if you need anything else," and left.

However willful or eccentric Kate might have appeared to the staff at Shaw Sutton when she first moved in, everyone who came to know her at the agency had to admit that she worked like a demon thereafter. She arrived early, when the halls were quiet and freshly vacuumed by the night shift, and she left late, when she was seen to leave at all. Her studio was down a little-used hallway—for security reasons—and she suspected that Jess had told the account group not to bother her. She got few visitors, and that suited her fine.

Jess and his secretary Thelma had the combination to the safe, but Kate's hours rarely agreed with theirs. She took instant photographs of the jewelry to work from when she could not have the actual pieces before her. Photos were poor substitutes; they had none of the fire and presence of the real thing, much as photos of people could hardly replace flesh and blood. But she made do. Jess accommodated her as much as possible by bringing down the pieces when he arrived each morning—which was early— and taking them back just before he left—which was often very late. Other than those two scheduled times each day, he did not visit. Kate suspected that he made himself scarce for her comfort, so that she could settle in without the heavy threat of an executive looming over her. She appreciated this in theory, but wondered if it would be so terribly unpleasant to see him more often. . . .

Chapter Three

Even as Kate's initial sketches progressed into detailed studies, the opening of her show drew near. She tried to stow it in the back of her mind—the only obligation she had left was to turn up at the reception—but she suffered a persistent case of butterflies.

"Stage fright," Esme declared tartly. They were spending a rare leisurely Saturday afternoon shopping in Soho for Kate's gallery outfit. The opening was the next evening.

"I suppose so." Kate sighed. "I just wish I could hang my paintings and then disappear into the woods until they all sold or everybody got tired of discussing them."

"Ah, but that's not politic. The critics and the big collectors want to examine the artist as well as the art. You can do a lot toward creating a favorable reception for your work by how you present your-self."

"You ought to be some actor's agent, Esme. Or in public relations."

"I'm in advertising—same thing. Now, what image are you going for? Devastatingly sexy? In-triguingly exotic? Terrifyingly avant garde?"

"I'm leaning toward the avant garde—but not the 'terrifying' part. Just something sort of austere and dramatic."

"Well, okay, but I want to go on record as voting for sexy. Most critics and buyers are male."

"That's their problem."

Kate ended up with a black angora sweater dress that swelled out at the padded shoulders and tapered drastically to a tight circle around her knees. Jet beads sparkled in an ornate yoke and then glinted randomly over the rest of the dress. She found black seamed stockings and black patent-leather pumps with short, needle-sharp heels.

Sunday afternoon Esme came over and, in ex-change for the loan of some of her classical record albums, scraped Kate's hair into a sleek braid, wrapped it into a heavy, glossy figure eight at the back of her neck, and pinned on a big black velvet bow. The ends fluttered between her shoulder blades.

"Pretty good for someone who combs her hair with her fingers," Esme announced proudly, giving her own rough blond hair a few tugs to make it stand up more. "Now I'd better go home and do some-thing about myself so I won't disgrace you at the opening."

"Thanks, Esme. I'll return the favor sometime."

"You can return it now by telling me why you decided on the sexy look instead of the artsy one."

"I did no such thing! This is a very serious dress. Look, it covers me from neck to knees."

"Maybe so, but it's what it does in between that counts."

Kate jumped up and looked at herself in the standing mirror. True, the angora was a *bit* clingy, but no more so than the sweaters and T-shirts she slobbed around in. "I'm sorry, Esme; this dress is handsome, maybe even a tad grand, but it is not slinky."

"I said 'sexy,' not 'slinky.' But never mind. I was just trying to get a rise out of you—and I did. I wondered if you might be dressing for someone special—and I don't mean Brad Morrow."

"*Ben* Morrow. And for whom else would I be dressing? We know all the people Pete Ridley could have invited, and they're all married or horrible or gay."

"Not all of them. Jess Schuyler isn't any of the above."

"Jess Schuyler! Did Pete invite him?"

"They're old cronies. Jess is something of a collector."

"Oh, so that's how he knows Pete." Kate stared grumpily at her reflection, suddenly feeling much too hot in the dress. She was going to burn up at the opening. "He probably won't come. Why drive into the city on a Sunday if you don't have to? Why, he lives way out in . . . in . . . where *does* he live, anyway?"

"He lives on the Upper East Side of Manhattan. Must be fifteen minutes by cab."

"Oh. Well, I'm not interested in him, no matter what may be running through your manipulative little mind."

"You're a fool if you're not."

"A happy fool. And safe."

Esme just raised her eyebrow.

Kate began to enjoy herself that evening once she got into the swing of being social. Maybe Esme was right and she could pick this skill up if she worked hard enough. Certainly her outfit was well-received. She began to float around in it a little less self-consciously, feeling handsome and grand and less like someone who lived in painter's pants. Pete Ridley was pleased with her. He sidled over to her when she had detached herself from the crowd and murmured, "You're selling your paintings all by yourself, kid. Go to it."

"Speak English, Peter," she growled, wondering why she liked this bony, nervous man. He had an aggressive intensity that she wouldn't have put up with in anyone else. Perhaps it was because that aggression sold her paintings. . . .

"I mean, you look gorgeous, sweetie—real Joan Crawford. It's very positive. See, Sam's squirming around like someone's just dug him out from under a rock. His work's good, but he'll never convince anyone that *he's* an *artist*. Get my drift?"

"You think maybe I should do something dramatic and artistic right here in the middle of the gallery? Make an impression?"

He narrowed his filmy gray eyes at her and retreated a step. "That depends . . . No, you'd probably do something *too* dramatic."

"Okay, I'll restrain myself. Listen, Pete, has everyone come who's important? Everyone you'd like me to meet? I'd kind of like to abandon ship— go home, unwind, crawl back under my own rock . . ."

Pete pulled a small note pad from an interior jacket pocket, consulted it, and shook his head. "Hmmm . . . No, no, there's Glen Southern yet to come. And Francisco, hmmm . . . No, there are still a few more who promised they'd be here. You know how bigwigs are—keep everyone on pins and needles until they turn up at the last moment."

Kate nodded wearily and moved off to begin one more desultory round of chitchat. The name of another absentee occurred to her, as it had several times that evening: Jess Schuyler. She felt some regret that she, not Esme, had turned out to be right after all. The sight of his tall, commanding presence in the gallery would have brought up the heads of all the fancy, arty people who, she suspected, went to openings only for the free liquor. Well, it would be their loss. . . .

A tap on the shoulder made her swing around and find herself face-to-face with Ben.

"Hello, Ben. Glad you could come!" She thought guiltily that she had totally forgotten to expect him. Why was it so hard for her to keep Ben in the forefront of her mind, while Jess rode there like the figurehead of a ship? Ben was a nice man, a bit pompous and prone to push his interests onto her, but no more so than most men—a definite improvement over Andrew. She sighed, unable to answer herself.

"Kate, let me introduce you to two of my dearest friends—Ellen and Windsor Somerset. Windsor is on the faculty of the Anthropology Department at New York University, and Ellen rather dabbles in art, as they say."

Kate shook hands with the jumpy, birdlike woman and her husband, who was, if possible, even more musty than Ben. Ben, at least, had come up with a reasonable blue wool suit for the occasion, although a hint of argyle had crept into the tie, but his dearest friend had on an unendurably shabby camel corduroy jacket and slacks that could have been rented out as a costume for a movie about the 1930s.

Ignoring this, Kate concentrated on the wife, Ellen. "I'm so glad to meet you. Do you paint also?"

"No, not at all," the woman said, as she gazed about seeming flustered and intimidated. "I make arrangements of dried flowers."

Kate smiled gamely. "Perhaps you'd like to meet Sam Rizzo—he's the sculptor." She gestured toward the delicate little moving wire and glass pieces set about on pedestals. If the woman tried hard enough, Kate hoped, she could see some resemblance to dried flower arrangements. "Meanwhile, let me show you to the bar."

Having involved them in choosing their drinks and a selection of tantalizing little canapes catered by the Loaf of Bread and Thou uptown, Kate slipped away, saying she had just seen another of her guests arrive. Ben gave her a pained look, but she ignored him.

As if her fib had some special power, she turned toward the door and saw him—Jess. He had just come in from the breezy night. His cheeks were stung pink beneath the tan and the collar of his coat was drawn up, giving him a dashing, secret-agent appearance. Her heart gave a definite jolt and she forgot what she had been doing. An acquaintance nearby looked at her curiously and said, "Why, Kate, you look as if you'd seen a ghost. Who is that?"

"My boss," Kate replied, hurriedly trying to recover her composure. "I didn't expect him."

"I didn't know you had a job, dear." The woman frowned. She was a well-established patron of the arts who liked her beneficiaries to be properly bohemian and employed only at their art.

"It's a commission actually. A large one." This obviously relieved the patroness. Kate took advantage of the break in conversation to excuse herself. "I really must go pay my respects."

"Of course."

But as Kate wove her slow way through the crowd, misgivings gnawed at her. After the first jolt at seeing him, she had seen something else—he was not alone. His companion was, if possible, even more elegant and attractive than the blonde at Weeds. This one had delicately feathered auburn hair that floated about her white shoulders, and she wore a teal blue sheath dress with absolutely no back. Jess had just taken her coat and given it to the attendant. Kate felt an unpleasant heat steam through her when she saw Jess place his hand on the bare skin of that back. The redhead's cool eyes flickered over the scene of paintings and art lovers; she looked bored. What nerve! Kate thought in quick anger. Since Jess had brought the redhead, she should at least have *tried* to be interested—or look as if she were.

Kate closed in on them, braced by irritation. She suddenly felt she represented the entire art world and that it had been slighted by this boorish woman. Whatever *was* Jess Schuyler doing in her company?

"Good evening," Kate said. "I'm so glad you could come, Jess."

He beamed at her and pressed her hand with undisguised warmth. His eyes travelled over her appraisingly. She felt hot again.

"Kate Angel, may I present Cassandra."

The redhead extended a cool, white hand and smiled frostily. Kate frowned at a flickering memory —there was something about this woman . . . Oh, yes, this Cassandra was *the* Cassandra, the fashion model. Kate had seen her aristocratic, ice-white face on no less than three magazine covers in the previous month. Jess certainly chose from the upper echelons of female beauty, she observed with something akin to annoyance. Didn't he care for normal women, whose skin might actually respond to a touch?

"I'm delighted to meet you, Cassandra. Are you an art lover too?" Kate knew she had meant those impetuous words to be sarcastic, but the woman just continued to smile and her gaze drifted off past Kate's head.

Jess, ever diplomatic, stepped into the silence. "Where are your paintings, Kate? We'd particularly like to see them."

He meant it, she could tell. At least he meant that *he'd* particularly like to see them. A stirring of pleasure suffused her. "Oh, they're over there beyond that aluminum mobile. But you really should see the whole show. There are quite a few good pieces here. Perhaps you might be tempted into collecting contemporary work, Jess. The bar is there to the right—they're serving hors d'oeuvres as well. I'll leave you to wander around and form your own opinions. It was a pleasure to meet you, Cassandra."

Kate grinned and twirled away, hoping her carriage expressed total unconcern. But the fact was that she found herself subliminally aware of Jess and his companion every step of their route through the gallery. Emotion jarred her when she saw him halt next to Ben. The two men chatted with their respective companions, unaware of each other. The contrast was astounding. Ben looked like an overlarge, just awakened honey bear to Jess's pantherlike sleekness.

When Jess passed the mobile and entered the area where Kate's paintings hung, she experienced such an attack of nerves that she had to disappear into the back room where the caterers were unwrapping trays of canapés amid great racks of undisplayed paintings. Pete stood by his desk making his typically extravagant arm gestures at a puffy-faced man in an

ostentatious silk suit. Kate immediately recognized
him as a writer for *Art Times*—a particularly arrogant, opinionated man—and regretted the coward-
ice that had driven her in there. Pete had caught
sight of her and was waving her over. "Kate—Kate,
darling! Here's one of my brighter lights now,
Bruno. You can ask her yourself."

This served as a warning that there was a stiff, arty
discussion awaiting her and she inhaled deeply.

A quarter of an hour later, with the sense that she
had held her own but hadn't convinced old Bruno of
anything, Kate escaped them both and buried herself further among the racks of giant canvases. She
still needed a moment to herself before braving the
fray outside. She always liked the mingled smells of
paint, varnish, sawdust and plain New York City
dirt. She tiptoed through the aisles, careful not to
let her dress catch on any projecting nails. All
around her stood the products of many hours of labor and passion on the part of many unrecognized
artists. She felt as though she could breathe in their
actual inspiration if she stood still and let her
mind reach out far enough. She closed her eyes
and let the charged but serene atmosphere soak into
her.

"Kate?" The voice was library soft but instantly
recognizable. Jess was standing at the end of the
aisle, half lit by the spotlights strung high up on the
storeroom's rafters.

"Hi," she said, barely above a whisper. She felt
unexpectedly shy.

He slipped his hands into his pockets and strolled
down the aisle toward her smiling. "I was looking for
you out in the gallery."

"Oh. I get a little overwhelmed by all the socializ-
ing. It's very restorative back here."

"It *does* have a definite . . . ambience," he agreed, looking up at the cobwebs draped over the unused tops of the racks. "I have to leave shortly— we've got reservations at the Charade for dinner."

Kate wondered whether Cassandra wouldn't find that particular Soho bistro too unutterably arty, but she kept quiet.

"I didn't want to leave without telling you how much I like your paintings. Your work is going in a wonderful direction. I'm pretty smug about you working on Exquisites."

"Thank you, kind sir." She dropped a courtesy— as well as she could, hobbled by the narrow dress.

"You're a very talented woman."

"A very talented *artist.*"

"I stand corrected—'artist.'" He grinned mischievously. "But isn't it possible to be both?"

"I'm not sure," she replied, suddenly serious. "But I don't think so."

He raised his eyebrows in surprise. "I'm truly sorry to hear that come from you. I hope someday a man will persuade you otherwise."

"It was a man who formed my opinion in the first place."

"Then he should be taken out and shot."

"I agree." She grinned cheerfully, wishing she hadn't let the conversation plunge into such depths. Being near him was a tantalizing ordeal. He seemed to concentrate all that was fascinating in the world into his dark, shining person, and whatever had less magnetic power simply faded into nonexistence. She felt like telling him everything that troubled or inspired her—her fears, her dreams. She felt like telling him about Andrew. She almost *had.* She wanted to put one hand softly on the fabric of his sleeve, feel the living arm beneath, and speak to him on the level of flesh and blood and spirit instead of

the superficial social level to which they were re-
stricted. He seemed so far beyond, so superior to the
kind of worthless conversation that was expected at
a party like this.

A thoughtful, somewhat shy look had stolen
across his handsome face. His voice was soft and
surprisingly tentative. "Might a man give you a
congratulatory kiss?"

"Sure," she said, smiling, and tipped her face so
that he could easily reach her cheek.

Instead he caught her chin gently upon two fingertips and kissed her on the lips. It was an incredibly
light brush, like the touch of butterfly wings, but it
shook Kate out of the casual pose she had been able,
until then, to maintain. Her lips parted with an
inaudible gasp and her eyes opened wide and found
his still inches away, wearing a similarly surprised
look.

"That was just practice, you know," he murmured
roughly and, before either of them could think
better of it, he bent and kissed her again—harder.
Their only point of contact was his mouth on hers,
but Kate flushed from scalp to toes, felt his fragrant,
tingling breath spread heat through her like a wild-
fire. She hadn't expected this; she knew he hadn't
expected it either. She also knew that in one more
moment he would have to touch her, have to follow
this electric contact with his arms, his tongue, the
vibrant caress of his powerful body.

She stepped back slightly and freed them both. He
straightened almost painfully and looked at her from
beneath a troubled frown. "I'm sorry, Kate . . ."

"Sorry?"

"I never meant to take advantage of . . . our work
relationship."

"Oh . . ." She understood slowly. "Don't worry.
We're on my turf now and it's my celebration. I'd

feel cheated if I didn't receive some special attention, after all. Thank you.'' She had to destroy the erotic memory of that kiss without hurting him or making him angry. As well as she knew that they could not work together if they were lovers, she knew they couldn't be antagonists either. Oh, it would have been so much easier if he had never kissed her! She smiled sweetly. "I promise to be back to my nasty old self tomorrow."

"Fine," he replied. She couldn't decide if his tone had been a bit short or if she had just imagined it. He gazed at her for another moment, then pulled himself together visibly. "Goodnight, then, Kate." He turned and was gone.

"Goodnight," she called, but it came out as a whisper and, in his sudden absence, she found she was shaking.

Kate returned to Shaw Sutton the next day relieved that her work with the show was over but worried about her relationship with Jess. She wished she could know that she had normalized things between them, that she could go on with the paintings and not give him another thought. Unfortunately, he had left her with that unreadable look in his dark eyes. And there was also the problem of her own reaction. With sweet, sexy words and skillful caresses Andrew had never been able to do to her senses what Jess Schuyler had done the previous night with a fleeting, unplanned kiss. Each time she thought about it she forgot where she was and what she was doing—she grew warm and breathless. A woman on the uptown bus had asked whether she was sick.

She threw herself into her tried-and-true cure— work. She loved to work. She knew of no exhaustion so satisfying as that at the end of a long day of painting when she had wrestled an image, even just one spot of coherence, out of a chaotic canvas.

Looking forward to this, Kate chose one of her studies and blocked it out on a piece of gessoed linen that measured a brave three feet by four feet. The background colors went on in wide, bold strokes—black, dark blood-red, indigo, rich plum. Then she started solidifying the design with medium tones and crisper shadows.

By noontime her body's needs drove her to the employees' cafeteria. Her normally healthy appetite expanded wildly when she was working, to compensate for the long stretches she would work without stopping at all.

Just as she picked up her tray from the salad counter she saw Jess vanishing through the swinging doors of the dining room. Regret and relief conflicted within her. She would have to encounter him soon, but she was nervous about discovering what the tone of their future relationship would be. To her surprise, she found that her interest was being echoed by a group of young women behind her.

"Oops, Lindsay, you just missed our Fearless Leader," one teasing voice said.

Kate glanced around discreetly and identified Lindsay as a tiny, plump girl who couldn't have been more than twenty years old. She was ducking her head to hide a blush. Evidently she had a crush on Jess. Kate smiled in private understanding and kept one ear unconsciously cocked.

Lindsay was protesting. "Come on, you guys! I make one comment that I think he's good-looking and you're all over me."

"Hey, you're new here. When you're here a little longer you'll find out that as soon as a girl says she thinks Jess Schuyler is good-looking, she's got a crush on him. It's impossible simply to like his looks—it always progresses to worship. There's nothing to stop it—he's just so darned perfect."

Kate raised her eyebrows and transferred her tray to the cash-register line. The girls followed closely, and their conversation continued to be audible. A third was saying, "Yeah, it's not fair—he's handsome, he's polite—I've never heard of him putting pressure on a girl . . . you know what I mean."

"It's called sexual discrimination—forcing a female employee to offer sexual favors in exchange for advancement or job security."

"Thank you, Rita—attorney-at-law. Anyway, he's a sweetie with everybody. And do you know what he's done every Valentine's Day since he's been here?"

"What?"

"He's had a little chocolate heart delivered to every woman at the agency—they're wrapped in little satin boxes."

Lindsay sighed ecstatically. "That's so romantic."

"That's expensive!" Kate recognized Rita's dry voice. "I see the bill."

"A small investment in employee morale—he *does* make us work hard, you know."

Kate paid for her lunch and found a table to herself. It was through no doing of hers that the trio took the table next to her. She seemed fated to hear their chatter, even though she had missed one or two exchanges by the time they got settled. Lindsay was asking in a timid voice: "So, is he married?"

"Nah," Rita replied. "Playboy."

"No! Rita just means he dates—a lot."

Rita added, "All beautiful women, too."

"Anyone from the agency?"

"No, it's against his policy."

"It is?" Lindsay sounded crushed.

"I guess. Anyway, I've never heard of it. Maybe he doesn't like women in advertising."

"Hey, I don't blame him. My boss is an absolute hellcat. Thinks she has to go around with her claws out all the time or someone'll steal her memo pad right out from under her."

The subject slid from Jess to bosses, and Kate successfully tuned them out. So, Jess never dated his employees, huh? That clarified his remark about taking advantage of their work relationship. Was this a practice born of moral scruples or of practical experience? Did he fear to put unfair pressure on an employee or to jeopardize her efficiency? Kate had never seen a man so true to his ethics. Perhaps she shouldn't be so nervous about seeing him now that the opening was over.

Back in her studio, she stared at the canvas and she stared at the phone. If he was afraid of intimidating her as her boss, then any gesture should come from her. Inhaling deeply, she picked up the receiver and dialed.

"Schuyler." His voice sounded warm and rich, even over the telephone wires.

"Hi—I've started one of the canvases," she began shyly. "Want to see?"

He came down promptly and paused in the doorway until her smile of welcome invited him in. He was beautifully dressed in a dark blue pinstripe suit; she was covered in paint. She was hyperaware of the impulsive energy contained in that sleek form, but he *was* containing it. He was carefully casual, perfectly cordial. He examined the blotchy canvas with interest for several long moments, comparing it with the detailed sketch she had propped against the easel leg.

"So this is how they start?"

"Yep. Pretty awful, huh?" She laughed.

"I'd never presume to criticize something at this stage. I'm just fascinated to see how a work of art evolves."

"Then come back once in a while. You'll see—it starts out as an idea in your head and a mess on the canvas. But you follow it along making decisions—this is important, this isn't, this will work if I shift it over a little, oops—my original idea was wrong, so I'll have to change it. I don't guarantee it'll look like the sketch; in fact, that's one thing I'm sure of—it won't. You can't ever completely preplan something. You have to be flexible and let it emerge."

"Sounds like a pretty good approach to life as well," he remarked, eyes twinkling over his own attempt at philosophy.

"I'll bet you handle your ad campaigns like that. They're works of art."

He grimaced. "To an extent, I suppose. But they're also business. Any organic plan gets to a point where you have to set it in concrete and drive it through, no matter what obstacles you come upon or what flaws you discover in your plan."

"Hmmm . . . I think I have more fun," she said teasingly, happy that he still seemed comfortable around her. Everything might have been horrible, but it looked as if she and Jess were going to be all right.

"Maybe you do," he allowed agreeably. "Maybe I'll have to change my ways."

She woke up each day hungry for the painting ahead and invigorated by the molten colors of fall that she saw out her window. Jess had begun to drop by often at her studio at the agency. He would usually flip through her sketches—she kept jotting down little ideas as they occurred to her—and step back for a look at the canvas. She'd lean back in her high swivel chair, her feet propped up on the drawing table's brace. Then he would sit on the window sill and they would chat. He had a quirky, abundant sense of humor, and the few comments he let fall about advertising showed an awareness of its absurdity that Kate found extremely winning.

She enjoyed the busy pace of her work and counted on seeing him every day for those short, satisfying talks. None of it held the emotional turmoil of life and work with Andrew. In fact, nothing about Jess was like Andrew. Andrew Keene had been, and still was, by all reports, a cutthroat businessman—she saw it now that she was no longer enthralled by him. Jess, on the other hand, inspired nothing but praise in his colleagues. Oh, doubtless he had left a few bodies by the wayside in his climb to the top, but he seemed to have a particularly soft touch with people.

Andrew had taken all the credit for Kate's labor. Thus he was able to keep the clients Keene Angel had acquired—they didn't know Kate's importance in the company until it was too late for her, because by then Andrew had found other artists. Jess went out of his way to identify the people responsible for ideas and work. He liberally handed out recognition —in the form of praise, bonuses, raises, and promotions—to those of merit.

Then came the day Jess told Kate the date of their first presentation to the client. A storm of protest stirred inside her, but she had come to want to please him so much that she said nothing. He wanted one finished painting and comprehensive studies for the other two by the Monday of the next week; he told her this on a Wednesday. She estimated quickly even while she assured Jess that she'd be ready. She *would* be ready, she vowed silently, if it killed her.

That night she worked until her eyes refused to read the names on her paint tubes. Alizarin crimson looked like the title of a monster movie. So she lay down on a clean tarp, with her bulky sweater pushed into a pillow, and closed her eyes for a short nap.

Jess found her like that in the morning. "Good heavens, Kate! Have you been here all night? You're freezing!"

"Guess I dozed off. . . ." She could hardly talk or see from grogginess. His hand was warm on her arm. "I smell coffee."

He had a mug of it with him and, after propping her against a cabinet, he pressed it into her hands.

"Yuck," she complained.

She liked it half milk, he drank it black. "Anyone as stupid as you are hasn't got the right to complain about my coffee."

She frowned in annoyance and focused on him. He looked unbearably awake—all clear-eyed and crisp in a dark blue suit and pale blue shirt. "Why am I stupid?"

"For staying here all night. It's not safe."

"Do goblins come out at night or something?"

"Don't talk back. I don't want you ever to stay here by yourself past nine o'clock." She was about to accuse him of being high-handed when he fished around in his pocket and laid a key in her palm. "But if you do, you'd better sleep in the room next to my office—and *lock* it!" He sat back on his heels, glaring at her. She smiled sweetly. She hadn't quite come awake and was savoring the delightful vision of his concerned face so close to her own.

"Is that clear?" he demanded.

"Yes, boss."

He chuckled then, a lovely, throaty rumble, which made her smile even more. "Well, *you're* very pleased with yourself," he remarked.

"The painting is fun."

"Good. Now go home and get yourself some proper rest. I don't want to see you back here before afternoon, if *then*."

"Yes, boss."

"Don't giggle—it destroys your credibility. I'm putting you in a cab."

He set her on her feet, wrapped the sweater around her and, indeed, put her in a cab. She woke up fully during the ride home, filled with ideas for the painting. A shower, fresh clothes, and breakfast put her totally right. She was back at the agency by eleven, sneaking around so that Jess wouldn't see her.

She made good progress on the painting, finishing it by dinner time on Friday. She didn't need to take up his offer of overnight lodging. The key made her nervous. At first she had put it in a file drawer. That didn't seem secure enough, so she had clipped it onto her key ring. Then she remembered how many times she had left her own keys lying about. Finally she had strung it on a long chain and hung it around her neck.

Sunday morning she gave in to a fit of nerves and went back to Shaw Sutton to check the painting one last time. The four comps had been matted and framed by the art department and were stacked in a corner. The painting glistened wetly. She had used too much varnish in the paint for it to dry in less than a couple of weeks, but the result was a luster akin to the glossy enamels on the jewelry.

She stood and looked at it critically. Try as she might, she could think of no way to improve it. In several years, when her technique and her eye would have improved, this one would seem primitive and clumsy. But right now it looked good. It was a

three-by-four-foot homage to the beauty of shape
and color and light. Only after a long look did you
notice that it was also a necklace of black and gold
and turquoise on an unfocused background that
might be glistening black tile. Some painters would
have used an airbrush to get the fine effects of light.
She had relied on sensitively mixed color and deft
strokes of the brush.

She made one last call to Frank and Sully, making
sure they were ready to transport the wet painting to
the presentation Monday evening. In keeping with
the elegance of the client's product, Jess had booked
a room at the Parkside Hotel for a cocktail party.

Chapter Four

Before she left the agency on Sunday morning, she wandered past Esme's office. The blond art director was there, hunched over her drawing table, more wan and gray beneath the eyes than ever.

"Esme, why are you here?" Kate inquired solicitously.

The young woman looked up blearily. "The soda pop people hurried up their TV schedule—now the work is overlapping with Exquisites."

"You're doing two major campaigns at once?"

"Essentially. Not for long, though—Jess is taking the jewelry off my hands in a few days. I just have to hang on until then."

"Jeez, I hope he pays you well."

"He does . . . not *that* well, though."

"Who will be the new art director for my stuff?"

For some reason Esme's eyes slid momentarily

away from Kate's. She sounded evasive; Kate had
no idea why. "The owner of the graphics company
Shaw Sutton just bought. You won't have much to
do with him—your paintings are all phase one, and
I've done that part already. He's taking on phase
two, the spring collection."

Kate nodded, not caring particularly what would
happen that far ahead. She was so heavily enmeshed
in her current work she had no energy for speculation about the future.

Then Esme asked, "What are *you* doing here? I
looked in on your painting this morning and it
seemed to be done."

Kate propped herself against a file cabinet and ran
her fingers over one of Esme's fancy French drafting
tools. "It is. Everything's ready; I'm just like a
mother who has to keep checking on her sleeping
child, that's all. I was about to go home and pay a
few bills, wash out socks—real exciting stuff."

"What are you wearing to the presentation tomorrow?"

"Oh, I don't know . . . I figured that since it will
be all corporate types I ought to wear something a
bit toned down—respectable, even."

Esme raised her eyebrow in amusement. "Guess
you don't know much about Michel LeClerc."

"The owner of Exquisites? No. Is there something
to know?"

"He's one of the few genuine jet set playboys I've
ever met. Actually, he's calmed down a lot since he
became involved with one of his designers—Felice
Champollion, I believe—but you can bet he's still
got an eye for women. There's a little picture of him
in that magazine, if you're curious—under the Bos-
ton fern."

Kate slid the magazine out from under the plant,

noting with furtive pleasure that the damp pot had made a wrinkled ring on Cassandra's arch face on the cover. Esme directed her to the photo and Kate examined her client, trying to imagine the paunchy, redfaced man as a playboy. Money must do wonders for one's eligibility, she decided.

"Thanks for the scoop, Esme. At least I'll recognize him now—maybe that will flatter him." ·

No matter how off-handedly Kate had treated the information on LeClerc, Esme had planted a lively seed in her mind. She made one last detour through Shaw Sutton—to Jess's office. She felt like a thief, which she was about to become. He had taught her the combination to the wall safe so that she could get the jewelry out herself in case neither he nor Thelma was available. This time she stuffed the black, gold, and turquoise necklace and the long, jointed earrings that went with it deep into her pocketbook. She left a short note that said, "Don't worry—I've got them. See you Monday night. Kate."

Then she went shopping.

She didn't play the tape of her answering machine all day Monday—she didn't want to hear what Jess had to say about her making off with the jewelry. He was in every way a remarkably insightful man, but he was too noble. He thought the Exquisites people would buy the campaign for its purely aesthetic value. She didn't want to rely on that.

When the doorbell rang it sounded angry to her guilty conscience. She almost didn't answer, but knew she'd have to face Jess sometime. She pressed the intercom switch—it was Esme. Kate buzzed her through the front door.

The knock on her loft door was *definitely* angry. She braced herself and opened it, admitting a wildly dressed Esme with a murderous expression on her face.

"What do you think you're doing? Jess needs those pieces for the presenta . . . Oh." She stopped in her tracks and stared at Kate.

Kate felt, for once, worthy of stares. Though she counted herself no great beauty, this time she had come out right. Her black hair hung loose to her waist in shiny, rippling cascades. Around her long blue eyes she had drawn Egyptian lines with a black kohl stick. She had used warm honey and peach colors on her fair skin to harmonize subtly with the necklace's rich gold.

But it was the dress that she was counting on—it was simply a little slip of ivory silk. It had no sleeves, thin spaghetti straps, and no shape save what her body gave it. In the boutique high up on Madison Avenue she had admired it on the mannequin and asked the saleswoman dubiously, "But what do I wear under it?"

The woman had smiled an intimate, infinitely wise smile and replied, "Very expensive perfume."

Kate had compromised by adding silk stockings to the perfume. It was still a pretty risky outfit . . . and effective. Esme's "Oh!" told her that. She hoped Michel LeClerc would say, "Oh!" She wasn't sure what she hoped Jess would say.

"So that's your plan!" Esme's anger had vanished into appreciation.

"I seem to remember *someone* saying, 'You can do a lot toward creating a favorable reception for your work by how you present yourself.'"

"That must have been me—it has that indisputable ring of truth."

"I *hope* it's true. I've rather grown to like my job."

"I thought you would."

Kate had rarely been to the Parkside Hotel. She let Esme lead her surely through the throng in the lobby and tried not to stare around her too gauchely. They rode up in an elevator to the fourth floor. For an early Monday evening there seemed to be no lack of well-dressed guests strolling through the halls, clinking ice in their glasses. Kate clutched the front of her black, dolman-sleeved opera coat, keeping it closed about her neck, and willed herself not to fall over her spike-heeled ivory-tinted shoes.

The doors to the Vanderbilt Room were ajar, emitting the tentative noises of people who hadn't quite gotten comfortable with each other but were making progress.

Esme bent toward her just before she crossed the threshold and said, "You're on your own, kid." True to her word, she split off instantly and headed for someone she knew, giving Kate no convenient body to hide behind. She paused uncertainly inside the door, then spotted Jess halfway across the room, entertaining a well-groomed couple. The woman was chic—a bit past the bloom of youth, but handsome. The man was large and florid and familiar from the photo in Esme's magazine—it was LeClerc, and he was unabashedly staring at her.

After a fraction of a second, Jess turned to discover his client's source of absorption . . . and he froze. His eyes locked onto Kate as if he had never seen her before. Perhaps he hadn't. Ever since her show she had dressed in nothing but jeans and bulky sweaters, with little makeup and her hair caught back in a braid. Burning under his gaze, but determined to follow her plan, she started forward. Other curious glances had joined Jess's. She couldn't stop in self-consciousness now—she had to go through with it. She let the coat fall away from her neck, where lay the lovely stolen necklace. Then she let the coat slide from her shoulders until she could slip it off and gather it in one hand. She had timed herself well; one more step brought her to Jess, and she nonchalantly gave him the coat.

"Good evening, Jess." Her voice was steady.

Jess, for once, could not reply immediately, so she smiled warmly at the older woman and then at the owner of Exquisites. "I recognize Monsieur LeClerc. Bon soir, monsieur."

He bowed over her hand with suavely perfect manners, laughter twinkling in his dark hazel eyes. Was he amused by her appearance? "Enchanté. Jess, you told me I would be pleased by the format you created for the Exquisites line. If this young lady is an example of your creativity, I am indeed pleased!"

No, he was not amused by her, but rather, she guessed, by Jess. She had never seen Jess at such a loss, and apparently neither had LeClerc. The stricken man recovered with a barely perceptible jolt. He cleared his throat and addressed the older woman as courtesy required. "Madame Champollion, allow me to introduce our artist—Kate Angel."

So this was the Champollion whose name was stamped on the back of every piece—the jewelry designer!

"Charmed, mademoiselle."

Kate allowed her enthusiasm to break through her cool. "Oh, madame! Your designs are so wonderful —I have never worked from such beautiful models."

The woman laughed brightly. "Ah, I think you exaggerate—but I shall let you!"

LeClerc smiled benignly at his designer, then at

Kate. "We are so looking forward to the unveiling of your work—our mutual work, I will say."

Jess had taken Kate's elbow. "If you will excuse us for a moment. Kate and I must see about some final preparations." He led her at a leisurely pace through the room, nodding and greeting acquaintances. Only the firm pressure on her arm betrayed the fact that he had something urgent on his mind. Toward the back of the small hall groupings of tall potted trees obscured the coat-check room and the auxiliary room where the canapés got their last bit of garnish and the bartenders, their ice. He handed her coat to the check girl and pulled Kate into the clump of trees. They were effectively screened from the rest of the room. Jess's hand lingered on her arm, and he looked down at her uncertainly. Now that he had her alone he seemed to have no idea what to say to her. His eyes were filled with awe, with the beginnings of something more demanding. "You're very infuriating," he said. His voice was rough and barely louder than a murmur.

"Am I?" She could smell his warm, foresty cologne, feel the heat pour from him through the beautiful black dinner jacket. "My prerogative as a temperamental artist . . . and as a woman." She tried to smile blithely but found herself unnerved by a feeling she hadn't enjoyed even during the very best days with Andrew.

Jess stepped back the barest inch, breaking the spell that had been settling over her like a honey net. She inhaled. "You have to admit my underhanded little plot made an impression on LeClerc."

"Yes, it did," Jess agreed in a stronger voice. "But it wasn't necessary."

"No?" She smiled teasingly. "I just wanted to help you sell your campaign, Jess."

"Your *work* will sell the campaign, as it should.

You are a different story. . . . I thought you were determined to let your art speak for you."

"I thought you thought that someday I should try to be a woman as well. So—I'm trying."

His serious eyes traversed her form deliberately but with an element of reluctance, as if he would rather have been able to ignore her. She felt herself unbearably revealed in the dress—she had bathing suits that covered her more adequately, yet a timid, unexplored part of her felt proud. Jess Schuyler's gaze might travel where it pleased, it would find no fault. She felt beautiful before him in a way that was fresh and intoxicating—beautiful and expectant.

"My future as an advertising artist is riding on this after all, Jess. Give me a kiss for luck."

She had said it lightly, seeking the pleasant bantering mood that she was used to using with him. He did not respond lightly. With no warning he pulled her mouth to his. She gasped at his suddenness and tasted the fiery traces of brandy on his tongue. His lips were hard with an anger she had not expected. His arms slid around her sides and settled at her waist, crushing her to him with a strength that smacked of desperation. He had not wanted to kiss her, she realized. All this time, since the opening of her show, he had acted the part of friendly, easygoing employer while something had been building up in him, something that now made his arms like steel, his mouth hot and searching. He clutched her so closely she could feel her heart hammering against the silk shirt and into the warm expanse of his chest. Off balance, she let him take her weight on his hips and hard, muscular thighs. She could feel the passion coursing through him as if there were no fabric between them, not even skin. His lips and teeth captured hers and coaxed them to hunger until, when his tongue brought his rich, spicy taste to her mouth, she groaned softly with relief. She had snaked her arms around his neck, buried her fingers in his thick hair. Some dim, strident part of her protested that this was not her, not Kate. Kate would never do this. Another, deeper part of her, with the sleepy, ageless confidence of instinct, countered that yes, it was indeed Kate.

But it was Jess who tore them apart. He held her against him still, his eyes filled with such wonder that Kate was tempted to laugh. She did not; her breaths were so fast and shallow she would have choked. She was afraid that if he let her go she would fall; all her muscles were molten, her bones loose at the joints. Very, very slowly he set her on her feet, keeping his hands tight upon her arms as if something compelled him to hang on to her.

"I'm sorry," he rasped, emotion flushing the most surprising pink into his tawny cheeks.

She found a scrap of voice. "Don't give me any of that employer/employee nonsense, Jess Schuyler."

"No," he acquiesced. "But I . . . I . . . I've mussed you." He ran one finger under her lower lip and pulled it away tinged with peach. In fact, her lipstick was lightly smeared all over his own mouth. She was tempted to laugh, but she didn't. Rather, she pulled the spotless white handkerchief from his breast pocket and wiped the color from his lips.

"It's just not your shade—a little more bronze, perhaps." She smiled experimentally. If only he would lose that amazed look. *She* didn't know how to act; she had never before been swept off her feet like this. What did one do? Did one recover and go on as if nothing had happened? Was this a normal occurrence among adults who had not avoided the opposite sex for years?

"Say something, please," she whispered. All of a sudden her eyes were filling up. . . .

Her tears moved him to response. "I didn't mean to upset you, Kate. Oh, I'm such a fool! I knew if I ever touched you again this would happen. Please forgive me. Oh, sweet Kate, don't cry."

She was no longer in danger of tears, but she willingly let him kiss her lids and her hot cheeks, marvelling at the exquisite gentleness possible in such a big, powerful man. She would have trusted him with her life right then; she trusted his strength, his sensitivity. . . . He couldn't possibly belong to the same sex as Andrew—not even the same species.

"Jess, mon ami!" came a cheerful call from beyond the trees.

"Damn!" Jess swore. "Clients!" His eyes returned to Kate's uplifted face and shone upon it with the warmth of the summer sun. "We'll talk later?"

She nodded earnestly and felt his hands reluctantly slip from her shoulders. He gathered himself and left the little copse of trees. She heard his voice greet LeClerc, then they moved out of range.

Kate took in a great gasp of breath. Her evening bag containing her lipstick and powder had fallen to the floor. Unsteadily she picked it up and repaired the damage to her face. Were her lips really swollen or did she just feel them so, suddenly aware of them as a focus of Jess's compelling attention? Her dress, due to its simple design, had endured well; the fact that it had actually stayed in place now seemed remarkable, Jess had crushed her against him so suddenly. The strength in his arms! She would not ever want to test his anger if his affection could leave such red marks on her arms. She rubbed them, trying to even out the color.

She finally decided she was just stalling. She looked fine; no one would have cause to suspect anything had happened if she could only *behave* normally. Could she? Bracing herself, she rejoined

the milling guests, latching on to some account
people who had been pleasant to her in the past. She
did well, laughing and chatting, sipping wine moderately in a haze of exhilaration, recalling how Jess's
voice had shaken when he spoke to her, how his eyes
had burned when he looked at her.

Once she made the mistake of searching for a sight
of him in the crowd, and the intense look he
returned nearly undid her. He was attached to
LeClerc and Madame Champollion, and his expression seemed to say that she should join them. She
avoided doing so until he appeared unexpectedly by
her side and took her elbow. "Shall we begin the
official part of this evening?"

He led them all into a little screening room where
he and his head writer showed a slide presentation of
sample ads, location choices for commercials and
fashion layouts, shots of models wearing jewelry. He
talked about his concepts for this and future lines,
the market he was aiming for, the media he'd use.
Listening to Jess's rich, graceful voice in a darkened
room was one of the more pleasant ways Kate could
think of to spend an evening with a crowd of people.

She tried hard to relax and did fairly well until the
end, when her paintings and sketches were unveiled.
Madame Champollion had a few suggestions to
make about the visual tone of the campaign. LeClerc
expressed concern that his ads reach the media well
before Christmas. The very nature of these questions indicated that they had, in their hearts, bought
the campaign. Kate was so proud of Jess she thought
she would burst right there in front of everyone. She
smiled uncontrollably and followed him with her
eyes as he sent his guests back to the main room for
coffee.

Madame Champollion and Michel LeClerc mo-
nopolized Jess with their enthusiasm. He sent Kate a

small smile of apology, and she smiled back in reassurance. She longed to be near him again, only half believing that such an intense feeling could ignite in her twice in one evening and wishing to give it a test.

Unexpectedly Jess waved her back to join him. He had a look of delight on his face. Felice Champollion nodded at her pleasantly. LeClerc, the reputed playboy, beamed—Kate thought she detected a slight leer on his face but chose to ignore it.

"Kate," Jess began. "Felice and Michel have asked if, after your paintings are finished, you will stay on Exquisites Phase One as a consultant."

"Please say yes, mademoiselle," LeClerc begged melodramatically. "It would give me the greatest pleasure to put my hopes in your hands." He grasped both her hands, palms up, and then squeezed them together, his eyes rolling to the heavens. Kate suppressed a giggle. Then she glanced unsurely at the elegant designer. Felice Champollion rewarded her by saying mildly, "You have a lovely feel for the jewelry. Please do accept the position."

"Well . . . what about the proper art director?" Kate asked Jess.

"Esme would be glad of your help on phase one. And the art director for phase two is too new to dare to make objections."

"Ah!" LeClerc burst in. "If this new art director is a man, he will have *no* objections whatsoever."

Jess raised his eyebrows at that but made no comment. Kate was so flattered that she said yes without another moment's thought. Jess seemed relieved somehow, as if he had expected her to refuse. How could she? It was a remarkable and alluring offer.

Then LeClerc dragged Jess away to talk to one of Exquisites' lawyers. Madame Champollion excused herself to make a phone call, and Kate was left alone. She wandered carelessly through the party, her mind taken up by imaginings of the future. What had she gotten herself involved in, other than a new job, that is? Should she have somehow remained aloof from this fascinating man—the synthesis of all she admired and feared? *Could* she have kept aloof?

Preoccupied, she did not notice the man who blocked her path until he spoke. "Well, if it isn't my better half."

The familiar voice grated on her nerves. Her eyes widened in disbelief as she looked up and saw him. "Andrew!"

He stood in his typical adolescently cool slouch, thumbs hooked into the pockets of his fleecy yellow pullover. He wore a white sweater under that—he was always cold, physically and emotionally.

Though she leaned away irritably, he gave her a thin-lipped peck on the cheek. "You look prosperous, love." Prosperous more readily applied to him—prosperous and Soho chic. He wore full beige linen pants tucked into suede ankle boots. His baby-soft blond hair had been cut in one of the trendy styles, and the slight spikiness emphasized its ethereal color. "And so happy to see me," he drawled in his dry, mocking voice. His cold blue eyes still held that snakelike glitter. She had once thought he possessed some secret insight into the world, but now she realized that his mystery was built on craftiness.

Kate gritted her teeth. "What are you doing here? Do you roam from hotel to hotel, crashing parties?"

"My, my! The devious ideas you can come up with! Maybe I should have kept you on at the studio after all. Still bitter, pet?" He grinned maliciously.

Was she? The sight of him seared her with memories. How besotted with him she had been! Where had those old romantic notions come from? At art school she had been too easily impressed by his brilliance, then by his precocious success with Keene Angel. The cruel facet of his character had only begun to show later in the way he manipulated people, the way he trampled their feelings for the sake of a job. Of course, Kate had been the one most commonly manipulated and trampled.

"I've been too busy to be bitter, Andrew. I'm sure it came as a surprise to both of us that my life did not actually fall apart without you. And I'm *not* your 'pet.'"

"Oh, I like this nasty new Kate. You may just have a future in advertising after all."

"You see everything reflected in your own mirror, don't you? Not all successful people are nasty. I happen to be working for someone right now who proves that." She involuntarily located Jess across the room and let her eyes linger briefly on his handsome form. As if possessed of an extra sense, he met her eyes and smiled warmly. She turned back to Andrew, trying to disguise the softened expression of her face.

He raised his eyebrows significantly, and she knew he had seen through her. "Aha, so you're sweet on the Great God Schuyler! Well, it's certainly part of your pattern—though I would have thought him a bit too gray-flannel-suit for you. Just watch you don't smother him in your fairy-tale notions of honor and ethics, Kate—they're damned oppressive. Remember, no one gets to Jess Schuyler's position by being a bleeding heart."

Kate had stiffened angrily. "Is this just your typical warped speculation or are you some sort of an expert all of a sudden?"

"Not all of a sudden. I investigated Schuyler quite thoroughly before I sold Keene Angel to his corporation."

Her mouth fell open. "You sold Keene Angel?" She remembered the comments Jess and Esme had dropped about the graphics studio soon to be added to the agency. But Keene Angel?

"I did indeed—for a fat pile of cash and Shaw Sutton stock. And a big salary to stay on as executive art director."

Andrew Keene at Shaw Sutton! Oh, it was too much! Of all the agencies in New York, he had to wind up at hers. She knew she would never again walk into those silver gray offices with any ease whatsoever.

Andrew was laughing at her, his small, sharp teeth flashing palely in his white face. "You're not looking forward to the prospect of working with me on Exquisites Phase Two? Maybe I'll find some other artist then."

Kate could not reply adequately. Esme had *known.* Damn her! She had sat there at her drawing table just yesterday and made those vague references to "the owner of the graphics company Shaw Sutton just bought." Never a warning—nothing so simple as, "Just so you're prepared—the new art director's name is Andrew Keene. . . ." Doubtless Esme had been looking out for her own career, wary of doing anything to upset the artist she had been responsible for bringing into the project. Whom could Kate trust? If not a woman who had been her friend for years, what about an ambitious man who had somehow become president of a major company while still in his thirties? She had to be a fool to ignore reality just because the reminder had come from Andrew.

She *had* been ready to ignore reality, hadn't she?

All Jess Schuyler had needed to do was kiss her a couple of times and butter her up with that powerful charm, and she had been ready to commit herself to him—not just her labor, but her soul.

These bitter thoughts raced through her head like a ravaging fire, leaving behind char. Andrew watched her carefully. Without framing one last remark, Kate turned· and walked away. She didn't hear his sarcastic call or see the agency people who nodded to her. She felt as if she were dragging herself away from the edge of an abyss.

Out in the main hallway, uncomfortably in view of an occasional strolling couple, Kate pummelled the elevator call button. Her anger and humiliation threatened to boil out of her like fiery lava. The glass and gilt elevator doors opened, but the elevator was on its way up, stubbornly refusing to help her escape. Her frantic feeling had made her almost nauseous when she heard Jess's deep voice call from the direction of the presentation room.

"Kate!"

She made herself turn and face him. He was carrying her coat. The distress in his dark eyes nearly softened her; then she pulled herself together.

"Kate, why are you leaving? What's the matter?"

He sounded so sincere, so concerned! It tore her heart. Well, maybe he *was* sincere, but it made no difference. Maybe Andrew had at one time cared for her, but the stronger forces of his nature controlled him in the end. Jess would never give in to a personal consideration when he had a client to think of.

"Has something upset you?" He put his hands on her shoulders. Their tender pressure made her shudder with emotion.

For some reason, she couldn't tell him about Andrew—not of how he had hurt her, not even that she knew him. What could Jess do? Let her out of her contract? Fire Andrew? Neither was exactly likely, and the last thing she wanted was to endure Jess's scrutiny once he knew about her past.

"Not at all," she replied brittlely. "I'm just tired. I guess I don't have your stamina for this social whirl."

His eyes clouded. "This is business, Kate, not a social whirl. Michel and Felice would like you to come up to their suite and chat a bit."

"About Exquisites?"

"No, just chat. They're nice people; they want to get to know you."

"That sounds social to me. They already know my work—that ought to be enough."

Briefly his grip tightened, and she looked up with a tiny twinge of fear. His eyes held no threat, only disappointment. He let her go but continued to stand close enough so that she could feel his tension. "This isn't like you, Kate."

"How do you know what's like me and what's not?" she flared, unable to maintain the cool she knew she needed. "You don't know me at all."

He kept his voice low, trying to soften her stridency. "I thought we were coming to know one another just a bit. I had hoped we could continue."

She could hardly look at him as she forced out her next words. "I wouldn't want anything to get in the way of the work."

At this he stepped back. His movement made her jump more than if he had raised a hand to strike her. Anger suffused his eyes now—the anger of an even-tempered man finally roused. But there was more; there was hurt. "I see," he said coldly. "Then nothing shall."

He held her gaze for a moment, long enough so that she could not mistake the tinge of contempt that fell upon her. The treacherous part of her that had melted into his arms wanted desperately to explain, to beg his forgiveness, to see again respect in his eyes. Although they might never again be easy in each other's presence, she wished he would not continue to look at her as if she had just thrown off a disguise.

"Your elevator is here," he informed her. She saw with surprise that the doors had opened while she was writhing under his gaze, and now the uniformed operator waited expressionlessly for her to enter. Jess thrust the black coat into her sensationless fingers, turned brusquely, and left without a further word. His broad, straight back, unbending in the black dinner jacket, seemed like a wall rising between them. Kate clutched her own coat in sweating hands and forced herself into the waiting car.

Chapter Five

Entering Shaw Sutton the next morning was the hardest thing Kate had ever had to do. She knew she wasn't up to her usual strength—she had spent the night wrestling with a headache that had seemed to knot all her nerves into a choked, contorted bundle of pain. Her thoughts had been similarly turbulent. She had relived every moment of her trouble with Andrew, grimly amazed at how much detail had stayed with her. The feelings came back as if they had hoarded their strength awaiting this chance to strike. Two years before, the first sense of disbelief had quickly given way to the hurt of betrayal. Only slowly had come the realization that she had laid *herself* open for it. She had been unreasonable—the only type of man she had ever wanted was a fiery, creative person, driven enough to match and surpass her own commitment. And when she found that in

Andrew, she had then expected him to place her *above* his passion for his work. Where was the logic in that? What conceit she had had! Or perhaps it had just been innocence, an adolescent ideal of romance that could not exist in the real world.

Whatever her fault had been, she could excuse it in the young, starry-eyed Kate of the past but not in the Kate she was today. She had thought herself a bit wiser now, until Jess Schuyler had come along with his easy charm and strength, his disarming good looks and the open admiration in his eyes. Well, so she had momentarily lost her head. No damage had been done. She would live. He would live.

But she still had to have this talk with him. . . .

On the receptionist's desk Kate found a message addressed to her: "Please see Mr. Schuyler ASAP." She pressed her lips tightly together in irritation and went to her studio. The "please" could not disguise his peremptory tone. Always before, he had allowed her to think she was an equal partner in their work together; now he was taking the gloves off, letting her know that she was an employee after all and therefore subject to his orders.

She threw her coat carelessly over a cabinet and looked at the new linen cut and folded by her easel. Ordinarily the sight of all that fresh, crisp fabric would have inspired her with a glorious energy; now she felt only sullen resentment that two more paintings remained to tie her to Jess Schuyler.

Little as she liked going to see Jess, there would be no starting work until she had cleared up a few things with him. Grimly she headed for the elevator.

Thelma was puttering around watering plants. A bunch of white mums perked up her desk. Kate had never seen it without flowers of some sort. Today the warm, cheery outer office and the secretary's genial manner only set Kate further on edge.

"Good morning, dear," Thelma greeted her.

Kate was abrupt. "Is he in?"

"Yes, he's expecting you. Don't let him bother you, dear—he's a little off temper today."

That makes two of us, Kate commented silently. She gathered up her nerve and pushed open the doors to the inner office. If her entrance surprised Jess he didn't show it. He was perched casually on the credenza, staring moodily into a large-screen slide viewer. He looked as if he were in his own house—in place of a suit he wore casual black trousers, a loose, woolly black pullover with suede elbow patches and a crew neck from which poked the collar of a pale yellow sweater. Another person who could wear yellow, she noted disgustedly. But he did not look healthy today. The slatted sunlight falling warmly across him failed to disguise the dark shadows beneath his eyes and the way his cheeks were drawn with weary tension. He must have stayed up too late "chatting" with Felice and Michel, she thought with satisfaction.

He deliberately shut off the viewer and put the slide in its box before turning his attention to Kate. The look in his eyes froze her. Hardened as she had thought herself to the necessity of cooling off their relationship, she found that it hurt to see it already accomplished. Jess rose and seemed taller than ever, more massive and implacable. The tender, laughing Jess was gone, totally buried beneath this hard-eyed man. Kate realized with resentment that he frightened her. This would never do.

"Thank you for being so prompt, Kate. We have several items to discuss."

She decided to take the conversation into her own

hands. "Principal among them is the fact that I cannot work with Andrew Keene."

He raised his eyebrows sardonically. "Cannot?"

"Cannot. Will not. I don't know what you saw in him that recommended him for the Exquisites account, but they are not qualities that endear him to me."

"I see. Talent and energy are drawbacks?"

"Don't deliberately misunderstand me, Jess Schuyler. It takes more than talent and energy to run a successful company, doesn't it? And it's those other qualities that make him objectionable."

Following her outburst, the silence was terrible. Jess examined her from beneath straight, glowering brows as one would scrutinize a familiar enemy. That was odd, she thought. Antipathy she could understand, impatience, regret that he had hired her—but why that hint of sad resignation?

Slowly he walked around the work-piled desk. It took all her control not to back away, but he stopped several paces from her.

"So, is it your intention to quit the project?" Before she could answer he pressed on. "Because if it is, be assured that I will prevent you. We have a contract. More than that, you've already done too much work for me to completely replan the project around another set of paintings. You're stuck with this job whether your delicate sensibilities are injured or not. You made a commitment and you will fulfill it."

He finished in such an intense tone of warning that she gaped at him, breathless, for a moment. She recovered quickly, fired by indignation. "Save your lectures, President Schuyler. You presume far too much. Maybe you've worked with irresponsible artists before, or maybe you just have an overdeveloped paranoia, but don't dump your suspicions on me. As I told you from the beginning—I have never missed a deadline or turned in sloppy work, and I have most certainly never backed out of a commitment just because my 'delicate sensibilities' were injured." Instead of taking offense at her tirade, Jess seemed to lose some of the censure in his eyes. Emboldened, Kate continued in a calmer voice. "But we still have the problem of Andrew Keene. You cannot twist my words around to tie me into a commitment to *him*. Esme is the art director for this phase one stuff. I'll work with her—as artist and as consultant, whatever that may entail, but, as I understand it, *he* is taking over only phase two. Am I right?"

"Yes. But he'll be observing this first phase in order to use the work as a base for the next phase. That's only reasonable, don't you agree?"

"Then he can get all his information from Esme, not me. I don't need to see him." Her eyes blazed, daring him to disagree.

He disagreed. "I'm afraid there will be a few occasions when you'll have to endure him. But wait!" He put up a hand to stop her hot protest. "I'll do everything I can to make it easier for you. I'll keep him from bothering you in every way possible. Will you accept that?"

Knowing she had very little choice, Kate decided to be gracious. "Yes." Then she added, "Thank you."

Kate went doggedly back to her studio. Nailing stretchers together gave some release to the violent energy she felt building up inside her. The hard work of yanking the fabric and holding it while she maneuvered the staple gun helped distract her from a dangerous feeling that was suspiciously like regret. She struggled with the linen savagely until she scraped her knuckles and drew blood. Then she sat on the floor sucking them and started to cry.

Kate's future contact with Jess was brief and all business. From his imperturbable manner no one would ever have suspected that he harbored any complaints against her. He treated her with the same diplomacy that he used with anyone, with the one change that now he sent Thelma down to deliver and retrieve the jewelry. Only occasionally did Kate imagine she saw something in his face other than careful indifference. She didn't know what it was exactly, and she might have imagined it anyway.

Maybe he *didn't* have any complaints about her now that he was sure she'd finish the job. Maybe he had forgotten that moment of apparent passion as easily as one forgot what one had said to an uninteresting dinner partner. She hated that possibility. In a flash of bitter amusement she told herself that she was being nonsensical—she wanted him to pine for her as much as she wanted to erase from the face of the earth all memory of his passion.

She still found the work engrossing. Although the studies had been worked out in detail, bringing a painting up to its full potential was still an exhausting endeavor. As she hunted around in the depths of her second piece, searching for all its possible energy, she came to an unwilling realization—the exhilaration she felt when she found she had worked out some unexpected glory of color and light, that achievement bought with so much study and effort, was nearly as intense as what she had felt in Jess's arms—and *that* had been so effortless, so instinctive. So far, it seemed, she must choose one thing over the other. She chose.

One morning she entered Shaw Sutton and found

her studio full of men and video equipment; full, as well, of Andrew. He was with one of the louder and more offensive men from the Exquisites account group and they were gesturing and directing a couple of agency porters to move her stuff around.

She wasted no civility on them. "What the hell are you doing here?"

"Howdy, Katy," said the one called Ed "We're-all-friends-here." "Thought up a new angle on this painting thing, honey. Client's so tickled by you and your work we decided to make a record of the whole process—a documentary, you know. Every once in a while we'll come in, film you working, snap a few stills, get you to say a few words about art—that kind of junk."

She advanced, hands jammed tightly into the pockets of her jeans so she wouldn't punch anybody. Andrew lounged near the windows, the sun turning his hair into a corona of yellow. He smiled ferally and said nothing.

"This is *your* doing, isn't it, Andrew?" she demanded. "Well, here are a few words for your documentary!" And she swore such a streak Ed turned pale and Andrew laughed.

Ed started a soothing speech about how a pretty girl shouldn't be so camera shy, and so on, but he said it to her back. Without conscious plan, her feet propelled her down the long-unused route to Jess's office, her anger blanketing any misgivings she might have had about seeing him. She brushed heedlessly past the alarmed secretary, banged open the office doors and stormed in, her cheeks red, her braid whipping like a snake.

Jess started from behind his desk, but she had already charged forward and planted her fists rigidly upon it. He sat back down and waited.

"What makes you think that just because I'm doing work for this agency, I'll put up with any offensive, publicity-grubbing ploy your ad man's mind comes up with? I will *not* have my studio torn apart by your wrecking crews just so you can show home movies of me to *Michel!*"

He listened to a few bursts of this sort of thing and then, when she had to catch her breath, replied quietly, "What are you talking about?"

His ignorance sounded sincere, she had to admit. She took herself in hand. "You promised you'd keep Andrew Keene away from me. He and that Ed what's-his-name are down there turning my studio into Twentieth Century Fox. I want them out!"

"Then they'll leave." He got up calmly, put on his jacket, and gestured for her to lead on. Though she had found no argument, she didn't know how to taper off her anger. It burned through her, making her feel upset but foolish. She led him to the scene of cameras and found a fugitive pleasure in the way he towered over Andrew. He thrust his hands in his pockets and lounged in the doorway, nodding amiably to each man in the room. "Morning. What's going on?"

Ed shot a disapproving look at Kate. "Well, you know how LeClerc's been itching to get in here and watch the girl paint—you've fended him off so far, but he's getting unhappy, Jess."

Kate raised her eyebrows. Jess had been displeasing his client for *her?* Ed continued. "We thought we'd sneak in now and then and pull together a film story on how the Exquisites campaign is rolling along. We've already got a piece down at the Ridley Gallery with that designer dame talking about Kate's other work . . ."

This was a surprise! Kate considered it in silence.

Jess shifted to another foot, his countenance still benign. "I don't think so. It's a nice idea, but we're not going to do it."

Ed's face fell. "What do you mean?"

"It disturbs the work. Do your peripheral pieces, but I'll have to say no to filming in here."

Ed grumbled but protested no further. He seemed to take Jess's word as law.

Andrew's expression was enigmatic. His pale eyes flickered from Jess to Kate and back. Jess regarded him with an equally unreadable manner. "As long as I've run into you, Andrew," he said, "Trip Solley has a few questions about one of the accounts you brought us. Could you stop by his office and help him out?"

Andrew languidly pushed himself off the window sill and strolled out, flawlessly casual. "On my way, boss." Kate wondered how much of what she heard was sarcasm and how much was just his usual cynical tone of voice.

Jess stood and waited while every last piece of camera equipment was hauled out and Kate's studio put back in its original condition. Then he turned her way and asked equably, "All right?"

She felt her face start to flush. "Yes."

"Good." And he left.

The sense that she had somehow wronged Jess by her anger stayed unpleasantly with Kate as she worked over the next several days. She didn't know how to correct it. When Felice Champollion called to take her to lunch one day, she accepted readily, feeling eager to be pleasant. The occasion proved to be a qualified delight. The designer had a sweet and genteel manner that made a new acquaintance with her comfortable. She was, in fact, much like Jess, though of course without that sexual element that complicated everything.

After lunch at the Parkside's terrace cafe they walked down Fifth Avenue. Felice, as she encouraged Kate to call her, wanted to pick up a little crystal apple from one of the posh stores. "For my daughter Giselle," she explained. "She is clumsy with fragile things but she loves beauty and must learn to handle it."

Kate watched as the tiny fruit was nestled in a cushioned satin box and considered this philosophy. "How old is Giselle?"

"Nearly sixteen and very wild for the young men." Felice smiled. "It is hard to think of them as 'young men' when they are all bony arms and legs and as gauche and silly as puppies. But somehow most of them do improve—and some even grow into exceptional men—*recherché*—like your Jess Schuyler. Oh, I have been tactless—he is not *your* Jess Schuyler, I think?"

Kate shook her head firmly, her heart beating hard and her mind flying back to search for whatever had caused Felice to make this mistake. She could only have gotten the idea at the presentation.

"I'm sorry. It seemed so fitting—I will see what I can do," Felice promised.

"Do? Oh, don't *do* anything. I'm happy with things just as they are . . . I'm seeing someone else," she said, lying and thinking how long it had been since old reliable Ben had called her.

Felice's black eyes narrowed skeptically. "*Ma chère,* you may be resigned, but you are *not* happy." She squinted at Kate. "No, you are not even resigned." Kate got no chance to argue; the woman had leaned down to massage her ankles. "I am not the athlete today. Let us have coffee somewhere."

Kate remembered a dessert shop on the East Side and directed a cab to it. Once there, Felice ordered expresso and an assortment of tiny tarts. Kate brooded while Felice chattered with the French waiter; before long Kate found that she had reduced two tarts to crumbs without eating anything.

"I think you are like my Giselle," her companion said severely.

"You mean being clumsy with beautiful things or being wild about young men?"

"Both! The first especially." She patted Kate's destructive hand maternally. "Listen, little one—I have had two husbands and several special friends who have not been husbands—I love beauty where I can find it. I enjoy it while it is given to me, and I am tender with it because I know it is perfectly capable of vanishing without my help."

"This has something to do with me?" Kate requested warily.

"Indeed. You make your art try to fill up the place in your heart that longs for a man." She swatted down Kate's angry retort. "No! Listen! Some women can pour themselves into work rather than love. And some pour themselves into love and give up the work. But *you*, Kate Angel, have too much passion in you to settle for just one of the two. Your work bears too much of your passion."

"That should make it better, more feeling . . ."

"But the feeling is tortured. You *want* to express beauty, but you are losing it to pain."

"This sounds too much like a romantic French novel, Felice."

"Scoff if you will. But think of my words when you next look at a half-done canvas. It will tell you the truth. The muscles in your back and in your arms when you hold the brush will tell you the truth."

Felice let the discussion end there, but the rest of

their visit was difficult. Kate felt stripped and poked into. Felice laced her light conversation with references to her many happy love affairs, which had all, evidently, flourished for their brief span and then ended in sweetness. Kate ground her teeth.

Esme's acerbic company was welcome that evening when they met for dinner in the agency's cafeteria.

"You look horrible, kid," Esme announced.

"This from a friend and fellow artist? You can't find some redeeming aesthetic value in my hellish appearance?"

"Sure, but El Greco already painted the world's quota of gaunt, yellow-faced people. You're working too hard."

"I'm working too hard on *your* account. It's a tough deadline, Esme. I'm barely going to squeak through if I can avoid all disasters."

"I told you you'd love it," Esme said provokingly. "Have a pork chop."

"That's a pork chop? I thought it was one of my old water color sponges."

"Yeah—Jess has done a lot with this agency, but I guess improving the food is beyond even *him*."

Kate's first task under her vague new job as consultant was to attend a special fashion show arranged to display the clothes that would be worn in the photo ads.

"What do I know about fashion?" she complained to Esme the afternoon of the event.

Esme, harried to the point where her eyes stared out of her head like eggs, grumbled back, "You know as much as anyone else who's going to be there. Look, just approach it like a painting. And don't worry a whole lot—this is more a little treat for the account people than a serious work session, though we *can* get a lot done if we try. You know—champagne, canapés, models walking around. Just enjoy yourself."

Kate agreed to worry less and Esme was satisfied. Then Kate asked in a dark voice, "Is Andrew going to be there?"

Esme fixed her with a pointed glare. "Probably. You're not going to flip out on me, are you?"

"Certainly not. I just like to be prepared."

"I'll sit between you."

"You'd better put a *wall* between us."

Esme made a sour face and Kate shut up.

Chapter Six

Jess had taste, Kate acknowledged reluctantly that evening. The bare features of the showroom were quietly decorated with beautiful vases of flowers. The tables along the runway bore linen tablecloths and little trays of delicate fruits and cheeses. Kate and Esme arrived shortly after the others from Shaw Sutton and chose a table well removed from both of the men Kate wished to avoid. Andrew had brought a doe-eyed young woman who fidgeted unconvincingly with a sketch pad. It was not the redheaded graphics student who had unseated Kate. How many women had Andrew gone through in two years? He ignored the girl from the time Kate noticed him until they left.

Jess sat with Felice and Michel. The Frenchman had already made quite a bit of headway on a bottle of champagne. Jess sipped his own drink moderately, and his dark eyes kept vigilant watch on the proceedings. Kate felt those eyes settle on her briefly and glance away. The memory of her tantrum over the camera incident and his calm response made her nearly squirm with discomfort. She wouldn't have called it guilt exactly, but the idea had begun to take root in her that she could probably act a little more decently toward him.

She was just running this over in her mind when Felice turned from smiling at Jess and leveled a significant glance at Kate. Kate looked away. She did not need eccentric Frenchwomen tutoring her in how to behave with men. She and Felice were different people. Felice might be able to tolerate love affairs that came and went like guests; Kate wanted a dedicated relationship or none—the kind of commitment in love that Jess required so adamantly in work.

Kate crossed her arms over her chest and prayed for the lights to dim. She could not bear the sight on either side of her—Jess, solid and handsome in his dark gray suit with a dove gray tie, or Andrew, with his fine profile turned away from his lost little girl friend.

For a time the clothes took her mind off men. Esme had chosen designers she thought sympathetic to the jewelry, and tonight their preliminary selections were ready for view. The problem was to narrow down the choices to the perfect outfits.

"Oh, Esme," Kate whispered reverently. "I can't possibly weed out the rejects. Everything is stunning."

"Well, *I* certainly can't—I'm so familiar with this stuff that I can't even see it clearly anymore. So, if you won't make the choices, someone *else* will." Her emphasis made Kate think immediately of Andrew. A furtive glance toward his table showed him grinning appreciatively at the models who swirled past him. With that incentive Kate settled determinedly to work. She chose all silks of rich gold, flawless white, pumpkin and silver, vivid aquamarine—the colors of the jewelry expanded to bold, body-sized sweeps of drama.

Esme bent toward her during the show and said, "I don't think we'll be able to outdo your little trick with that ivory silk dress, Kate. The look on Jess's face that night is exactly what I'd like to see on everyone who opens to a page with one of our ads."

Kate blushed in the darkness. How she wished she had gone to that presentation with her head in a sack. She never would have ended up seeing Andrew or obliging herself to continue on as a consultant . . . or kissing Jess Schuyler.

Instead of mentioning any of this she replied, "I hardly think that dress would fit these models, Esme. I must have twenty pounds on any of them."

"Hardly . . ." Then Esme examined her critically and corrected herself. "Well, maybe ten—but you're flesh and blood; they're practically hangers with legs. Look at them—anyone who thinks models are stunning should come to one of these shows. These women are all makeup and hair spray and clothes. Why, they're not even pretty—except for that blonde." Esme frowned suspiciously. "Wait a minute . . . my word! It's Genevieve Foucault! What's she doing pounding down a runway like some modeling student?"

"What do you mean?"

"I mean she's *big time*—she's been on so many magazine covers I can't even list all the names in one evening. This is really beneath her."

"Hey! It's honest work, isn't it?"

Esme contradicted her dryly. "It's hardly Italian *Vogue*."

Kate subsided, choosing rather to study this celebrity, Genevieve Foucault. The woman had come out in a shimmering red pajama suit that, while not one of Kate's choices for the ads, was immensely flattering to her. She had the most classic features Kate had ever seen—a thin, straight nose with delicately flaring nostrils, wide-swept cheeks that swelled over dramatically gaunt hollows. Her mouth was full and painted a bold, sensuous red, and her enormous blue eyes had deep, sleepy lids. She gave no hint of a smile and moved with icy, aristocratic grace. Kate couldn't take her eyes off of the woman, but some odd impression lingered to give her a chill. On a magazine cover, Genevieve Foucault would be glorious, but Kate had never felt comfortable with that kind of perfect, almost nonhuman beauty.

"She's really something!" Kate whispered.

A frown lay on her friend's face. "Yeah, she is. I wonder what's going on . . ."

Since Kate knew nothing about the modeling world, Esme's suspicions meant nothing to her. She watched the woman glide bonelessly away; then she put her notes in order.

The second part of the show was much more informal. Felice came over to join Kate and Esme, and they tallied their choices. After a very few minutes of discussion they had roughed out a selection and sent the list back to the dressing room.

"What happens now?" Kate inquired.

"Ah! The fun begins," Felice informed her in a cheery voice. "It is a bit like playing with dolls, is it not, Esme?"

"Esme never played with dolls." Kate laughed. "I think she was born with a drafting pen in one hand and a matt knife in the other."

Esme refused to be teased and steered the designer into a serious discussion. Kate's attention wandered. It didn't have to wander far before it flickered over her employer. He had remained with LeClerc and seemed to be showing him the rough drafts of copy, probably for the print ads. He had such a sure way about him, even while laying out his labors for a client's criticism. No nervousness showed on the calm, almost stern face, no fawning smile or nervous pallor. Michel read sheet after sheet, his own beefy face lighting up with glee. He clouted Jess on the shoulder when he was through. Jess allowed himself a modest smile and a nod of satisfaction. Then, as if he knew just where she was without searching, his eyes rose smoothly to Kate's. She dropped off her own guiltily. Out of the corner of her eye she saw him extract a cigarette from a slender gold case and light it. He smoked cigarettes? Somehow that bothered her more than the fact that he smoked a pipe. It seemed unhealthy. Wait a minute—why did she care whether he smoked or not?

With the lights up the models returned wearing the garments Kate and the others had specified. Felice jumped up to call to one of the dressers, "No, no! Come take away this scarf, *ma chère!*" She unwrapped the cloth from the model's neck and let it fall into the assistant's arms. "Let's try the square choker with this dress. Come, come—over here. What do you think, Kate?"

Kate joined her and was soon involved in repinning sashes and switching jewelry while she and her two colleagues discussed the effects. It was engrossing work; she hardly noticed that most of the Shaw Sutton people had trickled out of the hall as soon as the official show was over. The account group had been invited mostly as a courtesy, so that they could keep in touch with every aspect of the campaign and wouldn't feel left out. They weren't actually needed for the visual angle, and they knew it.

When she had half a moment to think idle thoughts, Kate let her eyes rove across the room. Jess had cleared his table of extraneous items and had unrolled some ad layouts. Michel perused them eagerly while, to her disgust, Andrew bent his slender form over the sheaf, holding forth with his own opinion. LeClerc and Jess listened attentively. Kate chewed her lip in distraction. It bothered her that Jess would listen to what Andrew had to say on any subject. The fact that Jess had presumably kept Andrew on as art director because he liked his work made no difference to the way Kate felt.

Did she see just the trace of a frown shadow Jess's features as he listened? No, Kate, she chided herself. You're just eager to think Jess Schuyler is better than he is. Of course he can work with Andrew—he's a professional; he can work with anyone. In fact, you'd do well to follow his example, she admitted to herself, though she knew that such an attitude was far beyond her.

At that moment, Andrew made a beeline for Genevieve Foucault. Attired in a tuxedo-jacketed white evening gown with her ash blond hair swept up over her head in loose curls, she looked polished and ultrasophisticated, way out of Andrew's class. Kate watched with cynical interest as he intersected her path and turned on his charm, such as he had. Genevieve did not look charmed. She listened expressionlessly, allowing every inch of her high-heeled height to pull her up over Andrew's head. After a moment her cool eyes strayed from Andrew's eager face, focused on something else, and stayed there. What would capture the interest of this beautiful woman? Curious, Kate followed her line of sight—to Jess. She stiffened. Kate paid no more attention to Andrew than did Genevieve as the model resumed her interrupted progress.

Esme appeared at Kate's side holding a choice of bracelets. "Kate, with the aqua dress do you think . . ." She paused and peered at her friend. Kate did not divert her attention quickly enough to hide where she had been looking. Esme breathed an "Oh" of understanding. "We come upon a familiar sight—Jess Schuyler and a beautiful woman. . . . Kate, you look as if you want to kill someone and, from what I've heard around the agency, my first guess is that it would be Jess. But maybe not . . ."

Kate's head snapped around, eyes widened in horror. The information that her relationship with Jess, whatever it was, had been the subject of talk "around the agency" appalled her. "Esme, I don't know what you're thinking, but . . ."

"Save it for strangers, hon. This is Esme, remember—your friend? I've been very careful to plant the information that you and Jess have only artistic conflicts."

Kate was not mollified. "Well, that's all we do have. And I don't know why you should think it's necessary to tell anyone anything."

Esme shrugged her shoulders and muttered, "If that's the way you want it to be . . . On the brighter side, look at Andrew—the man scorned. He's gone back to his little girl friend, but he looks angry!"

"So does she."

"Yeah, but I wonder if she'll give him hell when they get home. Somehow I don't think she's got as much spunk as you have."

"I never gave Andrew hell."

"You were young and innocent then. You'd do it now."

"I'll say," Kate mumbled under her breath. She tried to use the interruption to break her concentration on Jess's response to Genevieve, but it was ineffective. Genevieve had reached the small group formed of Jess, Michel, and another man from the account group. She said something that caused Jess to turn around; she smiled winningly. His face was a mask. Kate felt her arm being tugged, and she jerked around to see Felice casting a kindly look upon her. "Tell us, Kate—the golds in your paintings —are they very metallic?" Kate was soon immersed again in a discussion of the last few details. The three of them kept at it until they felt they had a wardrobe that would work for the campaign. The models gratefully headed for the dressing rooms and, tote bags over their shoulders, could soon be seen departing through the rear doors.

All but Genevieve Foucault. She reemerged from the back, as immaculately put together as ever, although this time she wore only a loosely fitted suit of cobalt blue wool. Kate was watching her with an inexplicable sensation of annoyance when she realized that Jess had crossed the room and turned up at her own elbow. Genevieve cut an unerring path toward him. Unwillingly, Kate heard every syllable of their brief and puzzling exchange.

The model said in a silky, pouting voice, tinted by a French accent, "So, Jess, you will drive me to my hotel, yes? It will be delightful to reminisce."

Reminisce? Kate wondered.

Jess replied in a curiously flat voice, "I'm sorry, Gen, no. I've already promised that I'd see Kate home."

What? Kate pivoted reflexively and opened her mouth. Jess gave her a look that killed the immediate denial on her lips—a look she would have been hard put to explain but struck her as entreaty. She decided she must have misread him and mumbled, "I'm more than happy to take a cab, Jess. If you two are old friends . . ." The phrase stuck in her throat.

"Nonsense. A promise is a promise," he declared firmly.

Even one you never made? she mused silently. She could hardly call her boss a liar in front of everybody, especially since she sensed there was much more beneath the surface of his untruth than she understood.

Genevieve leveled at Kate slitted blue eyes that could have frozen lava. In utter contrast, her voice came out sweet and cajoling. "I don't mind a detour. . . . I'm sure—eh, *Kate*, is it?—lives in a very picturesque part of the city . . ."

Jess cut her off. "I still have the Jaguar, Gen. I'd have to put you in the boot."

Genevieve Foucault pursed her lips in a manner that robbed them of every provocative curve. The darkness seemed to deepen beneath her classic cheekbones. Before her displeasure could show more overtly, Felice interposed herself between the model and Jess.

"Mademoiselle, I have a thought—Michel could offer you a lift. I must stay behind to fuss with things that bore him, and the poor man is desperate for rescue. Would you accept him as a substitute?"

Michel swept into view with a flourish that suited his wealth and dashing reputation, if not his build. Kate saw Genevieve's eyes tear reluctantly away from Jess and examine Michel suspiciously. *"Bon,"* she announced, slightly mollified.

Michel took her yellow leather satchel in one hand and gestured extravagantly toward the main doors with the other. The model cast a short, reluctant glance at Jess, but he did no more than nod and look pointedly at his watch.

As soon as the two were gone, Kate found Felice and Esme busily occupied, leaving her alone with this dark, unreadable man. He was not so unreadable now, though—he shifted uncomfortably, something she had never seen him do, and lifted a smile to her that was almost shy. "I hope you don't mind."

"Mind?" she endeavored to answer lightly. "Why should I mind a ride home? It's cheaper than a cab."

He looked a little pained, and she reminded herself abashedly that she was supposed to be nicer to him.

In the car a few minutes later, it took all her concentration not to notice his nearness and the tantalizing little attentions he paid her. In the underground garage she had felt his eyes follow her into the sleek, silver Jaguar. She told herself that the shiver that crossed her shoulders was due to the dampness of the garage.

Then, snug in the soft leather interior with Jess's strong hands on the wheel, she could no longer give herself that excuse. His eyes drifted thoughtfully to her as she sat stiffly on her own side of the car. A quiet, spicy cologne and the smells of wool, tobacco, and some indefinable essence played on her senses. She leaned her cheek against the window, seeking some antidote for the warmth she felt emanating from the man beside her. She remembered the way his body had poured out heat when he held her. Strangely, even now, after days and days of strain and pretended indifference, she felt the same kind of intensity about him, as if a single word or gesture from her could unleash all the passion held within him.

Imagination, Kate warned herself uneasily, glancing sideways at the source of her overheated thoughts. A normal person looking at him, she judged, would see a tall, graceful man, handsomer than most, alert but basically relaxed and confident. Why was it she insisted on seeing in him a cauldron of conflicting energies? Didn't she have anything better to do with her imagination?

"Are you too warm?" Jess inquired in a voice like glowing coals.

"Just tired," she replied shortly.

A jarring silence followed. Despite her intentions, she had once more been rude.

Jess cleared his throat and spoke again. "You work very hard. I apologize for my doubt. . . . It's ironic, but advertising has taught me to disbelieve most claims that are made for things. I'm right most of the time, but once in a while I *am* rough on something or someone who doesn't deserve it."

"Occupational hazard," she mumbled into her knuckles. Only the strictest attention to the street scene flashing by her window kept her from flinching under the candid look she knew he gave her. His look was as potent as a physical caress. "Don't worry about it," she finished.

This time he did not take her careless answer so well; she thought she could see the muscles in his arms and jaw bunch up as he swung the Jaguar onto Houston Street. Kate had to clutch the edge of the seat to keep herself from sliding onto the gear box. He hadn't driven this roughly all the way down through midtown and the Village, had he? Thank God they were almost to her home. Just the turn onto Greene Street and a couple of more blocks . . .

How did Jess know where she lived anyway? She had never told him. She opened her mouth and snapped it shut again. Did she really want to ask? Would it do her peace of mind any good to know that he had looked up her address in order to . . . to whatever? *No.*

"This is the building," she informed him even as he pulled into a space before it. She had reached for the door handle when she felt his hand press her arm. His chocolate brown, deep-lidded eyes met hers from barely a foot away. Her own inverted reflection sparkled in his black pupils.

"Humor me," he said firmly.

As she pondered what, exactly, he meant, he left the car, circled to her side, and efficiently handed her out. The deed had been accomplished before it occurred to Kate to scoff. Humor him in these old-fashioned little gestures of his? Is that what he meant? Lack of experience kept her from knowing whether she liked his manners or not.

Out on the steel plate that passed for sidewalk there in the old industrial section of Soho, Kate frowned. The friendly life of her neighborhood struck her abruptly—the two old, pink-haired women pulling shopping carts over the cobbled street, the strains of Vivaldi floating softly from a top-floor window, the bellows of delivery men around the corner. Here she was on her home turf, no longer an odd wheel in brushed steel gray offices on Madison Avenue. And Jess was with her. In the two or three seconds it took him to survey the street himself, she appraised him critically. Despite his beautiful black cashmere topcoat and the leather shoes that shone like onyx, he did not look out of place or even slightly uncomfortable with the eccentric character of her street. Indeed, he totally ignored the punky people beginning to stroll past on their evening rounds. He merely smiled and said a pleasant "Good evening" to Mrs. Lazar as she stood there with a sweater spilling over the collar of her balding mink coat and her cat pulling fretfully on its rhinestone harness.

Kate abandoned her speculation and headed for the door of her building. Jess got there before her and pulled at the big steel handle—unsuccessfully.

"We have locks down here in Soho," Kate informed him, unclipping her keys from her belt loop. "Probably as many as you have on the Upper East Side." She realized her mistake. Well, so they *each* knew where the other lived. . . .

"Upper *West* Side," he said, correcting her. "Seventy-fourth Street, between Columbus Avenue and the park. But, yes, we do have a lot of locks up there too."

He held the door for her, followed her in, and preceded her to the elevator.

"Then who sees you to your door when you go home?"

He smiled easily, although his eyes looked directly at her. "No one."

She nervously turned toward the green metal elevator cage. "Then you agree it's not a necessary practice?"

"No, I don't."

The car arrived and Jess dragged open the heavy grating with a crash that stripped Kate's nerves. She stalked inside and blocked him peevishly. "Why won't you admit that I know how to take care of myself?"

"I do admit it," he replied sincerely. "I'm just not sure that you always *do* take care of yourself."

"What does *that* mean?" she flared.

He braced the door open with both hands as it clattered, trying to close. In the poorly lit space that betrayed its industrial origin, he suddenly looked menacing, a commanding black shape radiating disapproval. She unwittingly backed further into the car. A harsh, nagging alarm went off and made her jump again. Jess let the door close behind him and the alarm stopped. "Top floor?"

"Yes." She stood, wary, as Jess formed a solid barrier between her and the exit. Something besides irritation rattled her, but it was the irritation that drove her to demand, "What do you mean I don't always take care of myself? Have I given you the impression that I expect someone else to do it for me?"

A dark, humorless chuckle sounded deep in his chest. "Hardly," he answered. Then, louder, he said, "I don't want to preach . . ."

"Then you should have stopped talking down in the lobby. But as long as you've started, please go on."

"All right, I will—I don't like the fact that you insist on judging me in terms of Andrew Keene."

She stiffened. "What do you mean?"

"I mean that I hired him for his professional credentials, not because I applaud his personal morals. I don't know exactly what he did to you— although he obviously did something—but I refuse to let you shut me out because of his mistakes. For God's sake, let me make my *own*."

"Feel free," she growled, wondering if the elevator had always been that slow. "But excuse me if *I* try to avoid them. I may have my differences with Andrew"—Jess raised his eyes at this understatement—"but I learned plenty from him. I learned what I could count on in my life, Jess Schuyler, and it's not men."

"Therefore you will never again feel anything for a man?"

She had started to tremble. "That's the idea."

"But that's not the reality, Kate. I won't believe that, there's too much at stake."

"What's at st . . ."

He stopped her with a light touch of his fingers on her lips. "Don't talk. You get us so tangled up when you talk."

Startled, she was unprepared for the elevator's rough halt. The jolt covered her compulsive move to grab the mesh of the elevator wall. She recovered in time to make a collected exit and hurried for her loft's door, dismayed to find Jess following only half a beat behind. Extremely rattled, she jammed her keys at the lock, missed, dropped them, and stood there shaking. She mumbled, afraid to raise her eyes, "You'd better settle for talking, Jess. It keeps me from hitting you."

"Is that our only other choice?"

She sensed his meaning but could not make herself react. Knowing she should be struggling, she stood absolutely still and felt his hands first search out the yielding curves of her back and then lift her off her feet. Her memory drowned her in the anticipation of his kiss a second before his lips captured hers. Her memory had been weak. One of his hands tangled itself wickedly in her hair and dragged her head back; his implacable arms kept her raised unsteadily on her toes, crushed into his chest, where her own hands curled in ineffectual little fists.

For a moment she looked straight into his eyes and saw that they were filled with an angry determination, the kind that could cow any business opposition. Then, in self-defense, she squeezed her eyes shut and concentrated on the ordeal of breathing. When was the last time she had inhaled? Her heart had long since pounded the air out of her lungs. She jerked backward and tore her hair from his fingers. As she gasped in pain he instantly loosened his grip and cradled the back of her head in his palm; but her relief was short-lived, for he took advantage of her opened mouth to kiss her more deeply. It worked. She unwillingly relaxed a trifle; her fingertips reached up to touch the warm skin of his neck and her mouth softened and welcomed the sweet caress of his tongue. Her head could not hold a thought. She felt as if the substance of her body had been changed—as cold, hard candle wax could be warmed to a soft, liquid texture.

She let him kiss her and pull her closer until it seemed their flesh must fuse. She felt the pulse in his neck throb an instant after his heart beat; she heard a rumble start low in his throat as he tried to speak her name; her own legs echoed the tremor she felt in his.

When he finally disengaged his mouth from hers, Jess murmured, "You're an artist, Kate—you can't kill such beauty. There's a part of you that's so generous, so warm, a part that wants to love."

His words gave her time to collect her wits. She wrenched around in his arms, achieving enough separation to look him coldly in the face. "Very neat," she remarked. "I tangle us up when *I* talk? All right, you've made your point, Mr. Psychoanalyst. But there's more to Kate than the past few seconds. Part of me *thinks*. I base my decisions on reason, not body heat."

He released her abruptly and stood back; warring emotions confused the expression on his handsome face. "Then I leave you to it. I hope you find reason a very comforting companion on long, lonely nights. I never have."

Rooted to the spot by shock, Kate watched him stride imperiously into the elevator, throw his weight on the control lever, and then descend out of sight amid a snarl of machinery.

She released her breath in one long, ragged gasp, surprised to find she had been holding it. A rush of angry tears made her grope for her keys and struggle blindly with the lock. The blurred sight of her homey loft failed to ease her unhappiness. What colossal nerve he had to judge her! He hadn't handled his life with perfect success either, or he wouldn't be divorced. And what did he know about lonely nights anyway—with his constant succession of beautiful companions? She knew what worked for her, and she knew what could drop her into desperate danger. Jess was the danger; that night he had merely proved it.

Chapter Seven

Jess stared out the window at a Manhattan muffled in gray mist. He had always thought of rain and fog as soft, comforting elements in a life that could occasionally be too bright, too hard edged. But that day the flattened, dreary colors only reinforced his somber mood. For several years, he realized, he had been too complacent—not careless or lazy, just overaccustomed to things going his way. He had put together an awesomely strong creative team at Shaw Sutton; obtained for them exciting, prestigious accounts, guided and focused them with the accuracy of a fine lens. His own ideas came fast and furious, his energy never faltered. He wrestled with business deals until they conformed to his own design. He had triumphed over all the pot-bellied old boys who ruled corporate affairs and who had predicted that his relative youth would ruin them. He had acquired responsibility and power until he knew he could run his company without interference.

Why did that all seem so minor? Why was he so restless? He had put his finger on the intercom button five times that morning to buzz Thelma, and each time he stopped short, unsure why he had wanted her. Once he thought it might have been to have her find Kate, but that idea made him even more frustrated. He had no real business with Kate—she was doubtless busily absorbed in the mysteries of her painting and would hardly welcome a summons. And what would they talk about? She had made it abundantly clear that she did not want his company.

Jess paced over the springy carpet, his entire body desperate for some movement that would take his full attention, make him feel as if he were *doing* something, even if it was only exhausting himself.

That woman! he fumed. *She* was doing this to him! He was used to understanding the world, anticipating its behavior and devising strategies to ensure his own advantage. But she defied understanding; she refused to yield to his knowledge of human nature or women or artists. That galled him. Only one thing had been consistent about her since the first cursed moment she had walked into his office—her passion to work. He could spot that kind of fire instantly—he had built his career on his ability to see such things. He knew she was worth the trouble she caused him. Her paintings had ignited a furnace of creative energy in the agency; each member of the Exquisites group strove to match her.

So that was one thing on which Jess could count. He stopped before his work-laden desk, momentarily mystified by the stacks of folders and memos awaiting his attention. His eyes strayed to the edge

of the wood surface where, for a few hours, some
days earlier, he had been able to make out faint
prints where her angry fingers had touched the desk
when she stormed in, furious about that camera
crew. The cleaning people had polished the wood
many times since then, but he imagined he could still
see the marks. His own hands clenched involuntarily. She had been consistent in one other area as
well—she tormented him as no woman ever had. He
had known many women more beautiful, but none
with that fierce spirit that lit her features with the
radiance he had seen in her. His experience with
women had not led him to expect a match to his own
intensity. Women had complex, tortuous minds, he
had found. Their desires and requirements were
often diametrically opposed to his and irreconcila-
ble. Only in a particularly bitter mood would he
have said women were fickle and shallow, but his
experience had not been good.

For a brief time, he thought he had seen something in Kate that was very like something in him.
And she *had* responded. She had melted into his
arms and offered her soul to him in every tender
gesture, every heart-tugging look. He had felt pre-
tense far too often to mistake the real thing.

And then she had closed up. Just like that. No
explanations, no reference to her earlier warmth,
just stony coldness and that lashing tongue accusing
him, or seeming to accuse him, of every sort of
offense. How had Andrew Keane wreaked so much
destruction on such a beautiful soul? It was difficult
to imagine that a shallow, obvious egotist such as
Keene could have any deep effect on Kate. Then
Jess got a vivid vision of a younger Kate, one still
dewy with the kind of idealistic innocence that was
the prerequisite for the cynicism she showed now.
He saw her impressed by Andrew—generously mis-

taking Keene's aggressiveness for inspiration, his cleverness for talent. Impressed? Clearly. But that would have been a relatively harmless disappointment for her to endure. Infatuated, perhaps? In love?

Furiously as his emotions denied this interpretation, his mind realized that it made a great many things fall into place. In the elevator to her loft he had spoken impulsively, driven by truths he only now realized. But what could he do to break down that ugly model she had built of the male sex? He had tried logic, he had tried passion, he had left her to her solitary devices, he had pressed her. A similar lack of progress would have made him abandon a business project for one more profitable; yet one thing held him to Kate implacably—every time he touched her that fire flowed. If only he could put her out of his mind, go back to predictable women, women who did not stir up such a conflagration.

Jess purposefully settled at his desk, determined to attack the work that no one else could do. Several accounts, particularly Exquisites, were building enormous momentum because of the approach of the Christmas season. At one time he could have immersed himself so thoroughly in agency matters that no woman would stand a chance of bothering him. He was afraid he would not escape so easily this time. Even laying aside the problem of Kate, he had to deal with the fact that Michel LeClerc, a good fellow but undisciplined, had decided that one of Exquisites models must be—and Jess groaned when the name scorched through his mind—Genevieve Foucault. No amount of rational argument had dissuaded the man. Genevieve's deteriorating reputation had not fazed him, Felice Champollion's possible displeasure had not worried him, and Jess's own pained expressions had not penetrated the

Frenchman's infatuation. Jess had done everything
he could short of sitting Michel down and running
him through the past six years. *That* Jess would
never do. His own personal problems were not his
client's concern. Michel was his client and if Michel
wanted Genevieve hired, Jess would hire her.

Sighing heavily, a weight descending on his shoulders, Jess reached for the phone.

Felice and Kate spent the morning after the fashion show roaming around Manhattan in a hired
limousine. Felice claimed that she needed a New
Yorker with her to keep the crooked merchants at
bay as she did her shopping, but Kate suspected that
the designer wanted to give her a little holiday. Kate
was grateful. The work had eaten up her energies to
the point where she was starting to feel hollow and a
bit strained at the seams. The deadline no longer
worried her. Although she couldn't take too many
days off for this sort of jaunt, only a major disaster
would prevent her from meeting her due date.

They picked up all the clothes for the campaign,
now cleaned and hung in dusty rose Exquisites
garment bags. These would be delivered to Shaw
Sutton's wardrobe mistress, in whose care they
would remain until the photo shoot. Then Felice
prowled through the jewelry stores in the diamond
district, surreptitiously sketching ideas that pleased
her. Then, for a dash of the exotic in jewelry design,
they visited a few specialty shops in Soho and the
Village. Felice bustled with energy—her enthusiasm
for gems and baubles never waned, and Kate had to
scurry to keep up.

Felice's habit of lunching in elegance took them to
a mirrored and gilded little cafe in Tribeca within
sight of the World Trade Center. Kate never tired of
the contrast between the unreal, shining perfection

of the twin towers and the dark, dingy warehouses of Tribeca which, as had happened in her beloved Soho, were being converted into luxury co-ops.

"Such a city of contrasts," Felice remarked, noticing the object of Kate's gaze. "Paris is soft and romantic, very comfortable for one as old and decrepit as I. But New York is for you young people who can run and run and run."

Kate laughed. "Considering who just did all that running and running, you should recast your theory!"

"No, I am right. I will collapse at the end of this campaign like a marionette whose strings have been cut, but you will still be dancing, *chère.*"

"Felice, I feel as if one more 'dance' would break my legs into splinters."

"Low blood sugar?" the Frenchwoman suggested uncertainly. "Or perhaps it is low biorhythms? I can never remember. You Americans are so fascinated with your health you have created a positive horror of afflictions. How much easier just to say that one is tired or unwell. Ah, here is the waiter to tell us what deliciously unhealthy things we can eat today."

Felice's name so suited her, Kate mused. She seemed free of the wildly swinging moods that beset Kate. How did one develop such a zest for life?

"You must have the squash soup, Kate. François assures me it is ambrosial."

Kate raised her eyebrows in a wry smile. Felice had fallen into instant camaraderie with yet another French waiter and, as usual, was determined to order the most fattening things on the menu. Kate acceded without a struggle. She had never aspired to be stick-thin—a fortunate choice, considering her build.

The soup came, with hot sweet potato bread and butter; a wonderfully bitter salad of spinach, watercress, and almonds; and, for the obligatory dessert, a Black Forest torte and coffee with Amaretto.

"I'd never be a model," Kate remarked, wondering if she could get up and walk after the meal.

"Or I. There is something very odd about women who can deny themselves constantly—when men would love them just as well with flesh on their bones. I suppose they rely on nonfattening pleasures." Her eyes narrowed, hinting at an unuttered thought.

Kate frowned over her own thoughts. She began tentatively, "That model yesterday . . ."

"Genevieve Foucault?"

"Yes! How did you know who I was going to ask about?"

"It is not hard, *ma petite*. She is a singular woman, that Genevieve. I have worked with her several times, and each experience has left me more and more amazed at what people will put up with from her."

"What do you mean?"

"Oh!" Felice cried in genuine exasperation. "She is wild! And irresponsible! She stays out all night with her . . . friends, though the word is too good for them . . . and then she misses jobs or comes in late looking as if she has been in the Bastille for a month. I would never hire her, but Michel is mad for her since he saw her yesterday."

"She's going to model the jewelry?" Kate demanded in amazement.

Felice ground her teeth and made an indistinct answer while she splashed coffee into her cup. She laced it by half with Amaretto and drank a large sip before she would speak more carefully. Kate was shocked at the venom she detected behind the woman's manner. "Michel enjoys women, my dear. I am used to him; I do not let his little flirtations bother me. But Genevieve Foucault is trouble for the *campaign*. I told him that and told him that, but he called Jess last night to ask for her. I fear it has been decided between them and done. We will have to shut up and deal with her ways—as women always have, alas!"

Jess's name brought Kate's head up sharply. She paled, her mind receiving a vivid picture of Genevieve's determined pursuit of him. In an unsteady voice she asked, "Does Jess know of Genevieve's reputation? Would he talk sense into Michel?"

Abruptly, Felice's glower was replaced by a tender-eyed look of concern. She reached across the tablecloth and laid her beringed hand on Kate's fingertips. "Ah, my dear—yes, he knows. He was married to her."

Kate could not speak. She suffered a momentary impression that the room had gone dark, and then fury rose in her throat like bile. Fury at what? At whom? She dreaded to think.

Felice rested her cheek upon her hand and gazed sadly at her young friend. *"Chère,* if you could look in the mirror right now, you would no longer try so hard to hide your feelings from yourself. Yes, they were married for a time and divorced two or three years ago. Jess is another one who likes beauty, though he is not, I think, as blinded by it as my foolish Michel. He is a passionate man, as you have seen, and very serious, very demanding. She is frivolous and selfish—and very *cold.*" Felice shuddered. "When I saw her step out last night I had a feeling . . . well, a bad feeling."

Kate had recovered her voice. "Esme was surprised to see her too. She said Genevieve was above doing jobs like that show, having done such glamorous work."

"That is true, although fewer and fewer people

have been willing to use her. I have not seen her in the major magazines for some time . . ." Her voice drifted off. "And I believe she has been involved with a fast crowd—you know the type—Monte Carlo, St. Tropez. A girl with beauty beyond her sense can get into a great deal of trouble . . ."

"Do you suppose that she's in financial trouble and *must* take this sort of work?"

Felice knitted her brows in perplexity. "Maybe . . . but there is something wrong with that idea. As silly as she is, Genevieve has class. She would somehow reinstate herself with the better clients . . . Madame Charbon at the Sylphide modeling agency has been just sick about the way the girl has ruined herself. Genevieve could go to her, I am sure, and start over. No, it is something else, the answer is in something specific about the job last night—the designers we used, the agency, Jess . . ." She stopped abruptly and her eyes slid quickly from Kate's.

The point, however, had been most surely made. In a quietly controlled voice Kate suggested, "She wants Jess back."

"That is just a guess, Kate, darling . . ."

"Which will be proven true or false in the near future. She will have ready access to him on the shoot."

"If Jess has hired her."

"If Jess has hired her."

Of course Jess had hired her. Kate didn't need to hear it from Esme to know it had happened—her heart told her. At the very best, he had hired her because his client had demanded it; at the worst, because there still existed some emotional connection between himself and his beautiful ex-wife.

Kate sat before her easel, slumped in an inattentive pose that worsened the strain in her shoulders. Badly mixed linseed oil dribbled from her palette into a greasy puddle on the floor. All her energy had been spent that afternoon *not* thinking about Jess and Genevieve. Between brush strokes her thoughts would stray toward them until she caught herself and sternly disciplined her mind. Then, a few minutes later, she'd drift off again. How had they met? Where had they lived? Why did they part? Why had Jess loved her? Kate thought back to every woman she had ever seen on Jess's arm—there had been the blonde at Weeds, redheaded Cassandra at the Ridley Gallery, and one or two others whom Kate had seen float from the inner office in high heels and silk dresses. Each and every one had been stunning— sophisticated, polished, and haughty. He certainly did seem to have a type, Kate thought glumly. And she certainly wasn't it.

She slapped down the brush, ignoring the resulting spatters of phthalo blue. She just hadn't been able to convince herself that she loathed Jess Schuyler. She *didn't* loathe him. Far from it. And it changed nothing—she still could not risk inviting the attentions of a man with all the qualifications to be despicable, no matter how charming his outer form.

Andrew's infiltration of Shaw Sutton was a blessing in disguise; every time she turned around she was reminded of how unscrupulous an ambitious man could be. The memory of his poor, miserable, wispy girl friend made Kate's temper steam. That was me once, she told herself sternly. But not again.

She needed to be around Esme, with her no-nonsense attitude; she needed to be wrapped up in her work so that none of this nonsense about men would bother her. Impatiently, Kate cleaned up her materials and went in search of her friend. A note on Esme's office door sent her to a conference room on the same floor. Sure enough, through the slightly opened doors, she saw Esme leaning over a huge table spread with layouts, color prints, type samples, and drafting equipment. Unfortunately, as Kate lifted her hand to push open the door, another figure came into view—Andrew. Kate struggled with a moment of hard resentment. Why did he always pop up like a poisonous mushroom? Kate hung back behind the door listening to Esme calmly and painstakingly explain the design of a series of Exquisites ads. Esme never let personal biases interfere with her job; she was a thorough professional. *Jess* was also a thorough professional. . . .

Kate took herself in hand and boldly threw open the door. Esme looked up with a vague smile, Andrew with a sneer disguised as a smile.

"Good timing, Kate," her friend said. "You're just the one we needed to talk to."

Kate strolled nonchalantly around the perimeter of the big oval table, eyes fixed on the layouts. "What's up?" she asked, pleased with the almost jolly tone she had managed to put into her voice.

Esme moved an orange plastic triangle over a detailed mechanical drawing as she answered. "Andrew has redesigned the Exquisites logo and come up with some gift boxes using your paintings as the main visual element."

"How clever of him—since only one of my paintings is finished."

She shouldn't have been so snide; she had only invited Andrew's even greater sarcasm. He curled his lip in his own skewed version of humor and remarked, "Well, I've got rather an intimate knowledge of your style, love. It isn't hard to figure out what you'll do in the future."

Kate met his malicious gaze with one of pure fire. How dare he bring up their past! How dare he imply that she was artistically predictable! Why, since leaving him (or his leaving her; it hardly mattered now), she had forged an entirely new, much stronger, more vigorous style. That he could even think he possessed the sensitivity to have the slightest inkling of how she painted!

Esme cleared her throat. Kate realized she had been bending a metal ruler between her hands. She released it and laid it down on the table, distorted into a boomerang. Esme examined it out of the corner of her eye but made no comment.

"How fortunate that we have a chance to work together again, Andrew," Kate said significantly. "I'd hate to let old impressions linger when I can develop a whole set of fresh ones."

Andrew frowned, not quite sure how to take that. A chuckle bubbled up from Esme, quickly disguised as a cough. The blonde determinedly distracted them. "Listen, Kate, if you could paint up some swatches of your main colors and the accents, I'll have the photo lab work on printing them and then everyone can have color samples to work from. Is that a big pain in the butt?"

"Not at all. You'll have to be careful, though—the oil paint takes a long time to dry the way I've mixed it."

Esme nodded. "Okay, I'll warn the lab. Well, that's all I needed to ask you officially. Would you like to look over Andrew's new ideas? They're good . . ." In her enthusiasm for the work, Esme had forgotten Kate's obvious aversion. She cut off her sentence, and the palest hint of a blush showed in her powdered cheeks.

Andrew laughed silently—his eyes were ice blue slits screened by unnaturally white lashes. "Maybe you would be more interested in the models who have been chosen for phase one." He added slyly, "I don't believe you were in on *those* discussions, Kate."

Esme had the grace to look uncomfortable while Andrew spread out a handful of large, glossy photos. One face jumped out at Kate—Genevieve. The photographer had caught her at her most china perfect—skin like white bisque, eyes like glittering blue diamonds. When Kate remained impassive, Andrew picked up that particular photo and held it admiringly. "I rather favor this girl, although she hardly suits the jewelry. Champollion designs for women more like . . . well, more like *you*, Kate. Really, her work is too . . . um . . . *primitive* for someone of Genevieve Foucault's refinement."

The taunt was too blatant, as well as unimaginative, for Kate to bother refuting it. She already had the satisfaction of knowing that Genevieve had walked past Andrew as if he were a potted plant. Even Esme frowned at him disgustedly. But Andrew, in his magnificent obliviousness, failed to see how badly he had handled his insult and went on. "If we artists had been responsible for choosing models, I know we would have passed on her, lovely as she is . . ." He nastily let the suggestion dangle.

Esme's dry manner held off Kate's retort. "You know very well LeClerc is in a total dither about her, Andrew. It doesn't take a genius to figure out *he* was Jess's reason for hiring the woman."

Andrew cast a pitying look upon them both, concentrating on Kate. "And of course it has nothing to do with the fact that Genevieve Foucault is Schuyler's wife?"

"*Ex*-wife," Esme and Kate said in unison.

He merely raised his slender eyebrows.

Andrew's intimations made Kate so angry she could no longer stay in the same room with him. She left, not sure if her little demonstration of patience had worked. She could still take him only in small doses. She took a brisk walk up Fifth Avenue past the Metropolitan Museum of Art and then down Madison Avenue, looking in all the posh shop windows. When Shaw Sutton came into view, her nervous energy had been disciplined into a readiness to work. She bought a sandwich and orange juice at a deli and went up to her studio.

By midnight she had finished the second painting. In the light of day she expected that she'd see some changes to be made, but at that moment she felt she had really gotten somewhere, really accomplished something. And she felt utterly spent. While looking at her canvas, she suddenly realized with a jolt that she'd literally been asleep on her feet for a moment —luckily not long enough for her to pitch forward into her painting. She put her brushes in turpentine to soak, scraped the clotted colors off her palette, and left the rest of the studio messy. She didn't even think she had the energy to find a cab; the floor began to look comfy. An image came to her mind of Jess's concerned face that morning when he had found her curled up on that same floor and given her the key to his private suite. She had pulled it from her neck and tossed it somewhere—the drawer in her taboret. She found it and stood looking at it, feeling the small, cold weight in her hand, like the one in her heart. Well, why the heck not. She shrugged. He had made the offer before any intimacy had grown or died between them. Avoiding the bed just because it was his was hardly a mature, rational way to get over that intimacy.

She staggered upstairs, half expecting to encounter Jess's secretary. Don't be absurd, Kate, she told herself. Secretaries don't work until midnight. The outer office was dark, empty and spooky. She crossed quickly into the large inner office. It too lay

empty of everything but furniture and the speckle of
city lights. Forcing herself to be very matter-of-fact,
she fit the key into the suite's door, pushed it open,
and entered. With the opening of the door a soft
light came on—a brass sconce on the wall seemed to
be connected to an automatic switch, although she
found a manual switch for it also just inside the door.
It gave just enough light to keep her from bumping
into things. She saw the smooth, flat shapes of the
big bed, the chairs, and the small tables. All was
deserted.

Somewhere, she expected, Jess had an alarm
clock. While she was still clearheaded she must find
it and set it for early enough the next morning to
make her escape unobserved. She hunted gingerly
through built-in drawers until she found it. There
were only a few things around that spoke of the
suite's proper inhabitant—the little wood and brass
clock, a small library of cassettes, a hardcover
biography of Lawrence of Arabia, the log cabin
quilt, a briar pipe, and a box holding bags of
tobacco.

She undressed and folded her clothes at the foot of
the bed. The bed was soft, the sheets silky and fresh.
She couldn't have been more tired, but sleep refused
to come. Maybe it was just the irony of the situation
that needled her—here she was in Jess Schuyler's
bed. Ha. She had never even been in Andrew's.

Recognizing the problem did not make it go away.
She fidgeted, feeling some subtle longing take root in
her—one related to the larger longing for him.
Finally she flung herself out of the bed and restlessly
padded the perimeter of the room. The cool air
raised goosebumps all over her. If only she had
brought a gown or a robe. She didn't own any
gowns, actually, just decrepit T-shirts for the very

coldest weather. At other times she found her bare
skin quite comfortable.

But she felt especially cold in Jess's suite. Perhaps
she could find a robe in the closet. . . . That was it!
Her longing was to poke through Jess's things. She
groaned at herself. At least she could satisfy that
longing quickly and harmlessly. The closet door
rolled back at her touch and little lights glowed
inside. The air smelled deliciously of cedar—a cedar
wardrobe, what a luxury! She stepped in. His suits
hung on padded hangers along a wooden rail. There
were quite a few; some were in dry-cleaning bags.
The uncovered ones showed the range of colors to
which he was partial—black, dark blue, muted bur-
gundy and mauve, ivory and cream, stark white.
Across the closet hung his shirts. They tended
toward delicate colors—white, pale blue, canary.
She yielded to her snobbery and read a few labels—
all designer shirts. She stood there naked, feeling the
gorgeous wools and silks slide over her arms and her
stomach. They smelled intoxicating; beneath the
cedar she caught whiffs of woodsy cologne and,
fainter still, a warm, tantalizing trace of a scent that
must have come from Jess's own glowing skin.

She decided there was something perverse about
torturing herself that way. She shut the closet and
threw herself into the bed. This time she slept . . .

. . . until the brass door light came on of itself and
a man's voice spoke to someone out in the office.
Jess's voice. She froze, half awake and wholly unprepared. He was muttering to the other person; now
he was turning . . . he looked toward the bed and
started perceptibly. Enough of her head protruded
from the covers so that he *must* recognize her—she
hoped. He said to his invisible companion, "Stay
here, I'll be out soon." Then he shut the door

between them, and the lights went out until he found the manual switch. "I'm sorry to disturb you," he said, his voice deep and velvety and very quiet. "I came back for something."

She struggled to sit upright and still keep the covers decently drawn up. She hadn't a scrap of clothing within range or she would have grabbed for it. She could feel herself flushing down to her toes. Normally she wasn't so self-conscious—she was an artist, used to the human body, particularly her own, which she had drawn so many times in the absence of a model. Having Jess not ten feet away from her in this night-dark room, her flesh warm and caressed by his sheets, and knowing the situation could have developed naturally if she had let it . . . all of it made her painfully shy.

She told herself that it did not matter how intently he looked at her, he could not actually see through the covers. Still, a thrill of danger ran through her. "If you need the room tonight, I'll leave," she offered. "Just give me a couple of minutes." Who *was* outside in the office anyway? A woman?

"No, no. I'll just pick up my watch."

"So? Go ahead. Where is it?"

"In the drawer on your side of the bed." Still he did not move.

"I'm not contagious," she growled.

With an unreadable expression on his face, he walked soundlessly over the carpet, his big body utterly sure in the dark. It was all she could do not to gasp when he towered over her and swiftly knelt by her. She gathered the covers a little tighter and watched him. He wore a new cologne—it was deeper, muskier. He looked so vividly alive and male that she wanted to reach out and stroke the smooth, flexible muscles of his back. She kept her hand still, restricting herself to the sight of his dim profile. His jaw was clenched, or was it a trick of the feeble light?

He soon found the watch in a velvet case and strapped it on his wrist. But he did not leave. He stood looking down at her with an expression on his face that caused her to shrink deeper into the pillows. His eyes held hers with the power of a snake charmer's even as he settled his weight on the bed next to her hip and braced one arm near her opposite shoulder. Her immediate reaction was to wriggle out from under his looming shadow, but she squelched it; the covers, pinned beneath him, would have stayed behind. She waited in suspense.

"Not contagious, Kate?" he murmured, his voice as rough and deep as a stormy sea. "Oh, but you are. Instantly and fatally contagious." His free hand floated feather light across her cheek, down her neck, out over her white shoulder, and then back to trace the line of her collarbone in fire. She made a tiny sound of distress that caused him to raise his eyebrows in dark amusement. "But since I'm already afflicted, it wouldn't do me much good to stay away, would it?"

Even more slowly his fingers trailed down to the edge of the sheet and pulled at it. She found her voice and said hoarsely, "Stop." But he leaned closer. As his lips found hers she felt the cold night air wash over her naked breasts, her stomach. His kisses were light and tantalizing, just urgent enough to keep her thoroughly occupied. His hand stole up to stroke one nipple lightly, and then nestle warmly over the soft curve of her breast. Her will betrayed her, treacherously letting her body throb with desire for his touch. In answer, he freed his other arm and slid both hands beneath her shoulders. Then he lowered his full weight onto her and let the movement change his teasing kisses to one of passion.

Sensation drove every rational thought from her mind; the chafe of his wool jacket against her skin, the commanding pressure of his body on hers, his intoxicating taste, the warm smell of his gorgeous skin, the silk of his hair curled around her fingers . . .

She barely heard the knock at the door, but she felt him stiffen and his mouth break away from hers.

"Jess?" came a muffled feminine voice. "Are you alive in there?" Then the doorknob rattled—he had locked it.

He looked down at Kate with heavy-lidded eyes that only slowly regained their focus. He whispered provokingly, "Sweet dreams, Kate." Then he dragged himself to his feet; the loss of his presence was almost a physical pain to Kate. He walked unhesitatingly to the door, turned out the dim light, and let himself out. For a few moments Kate heard a woman's complaining voice. He answered in soothing, casual tones. Kate curled herself into a shuddering ball, damning him viciously. Torment one woman, placate another—it seemed to be all in an evening's work to him. She thought she felt sick; she certainly felt wretched. Sweet dreams, indeed—there was no chance of that.

Chapter Eight

"Your half-done canvas will tell you the truth," Felice Champollion had said. "The muscles in your back and in your arms when you hold the brush will tell you the truth." Kate fixed her eyes on the canvas and begged it to tell her *something*. It was an utter chaos of color and partially defined shape. She referred to the sketch and saw the clear form of an earring running diagonally from one corner of the frame to the opposite corner. She looked back at her painting and saw nonsense. She couldn't make it congeal into any sort of image. Many paintings were like that—you fought them through their impossible stage and they turned out to be your best works— more profound, more complex than the others. Or they turned out to be garbage. She was afraid this one would insist on being garbage. And she couldn't afford to scrap it. Time was too short.

Frustration cramped the muscles in her back and arms. She winced and thought wryly, They're telling me to do yoga. That was the only dash of humor she had so far enjoyed that day. She felt tense—unable to concentrate, unable to coordinate her hands. She wondered whether she had contracted some disease of the nerves. It was an unfortunate thought; it reminded her of Jess's remarks to her on that incredible night in his suite. She had done a fairly good job of pretending that whole night hadn't happened, and certainly no word or look from Jess disproved her—indeed, he seemed to have evaporated from the face of the earth. *Fine,* she thought bad-temperedly.

Even the weather felt destructive. The first crack of thunder she heard through the double-paned glass caused her to jump like a scalded cat. Lightning tore through the steel gray sky—it looked as if it must be electrocuting some of the tall buildings between her and the curtain of overcast. Shortly afterward, she heard the faint whine of fire engines from the streets below.

Maybe Shaw Sutton will burn down, she brooded. Then I can go home and forget all this. But she couldn't forget it all even if Shaw Sutton were to burn down or New York fall into rubble, or even if the whole Northeast were to disappear into some blessed crustal fault. Her contract would still be in effect. Jess had sent her an interoffice memo detailing the photo shoot scheduled to begin in eight days' time. It was to be held, of all places, on some retired farm-cum-estate near Greenwich, Connecticut, and if Fairfield County didn't survive long enough for Jess's people to photograph all the jewelry, doubtless Jess had a hundred scenic places on tap to replace it.

Needing a break, Kate put her feet on the window

ledge and leaned back in the chair; her braid dusted the floorboards, picking up all manner of grunge, but she didn't care.

Esme, almost a permanent resident of the agency lately, answered her phone when Kate called. "Shaw Sutton Mausoleum."

"My sentiments exactly."

"Hi, Kate. What are you doing here in the middle of the night?"

"It's midafternoon. What we're in the middle of is a thundercloud."

"Oh. What day is it?"

"T minus eight days. And that's what I'm calling about—why am I going to this photo shoot for Exquisites?"

"Because you've always been fascinated by the world of high fashion?"

"Not likely."

"You need a paid vacation in God's country?"

"Greenwich?"

"No, huh? Okay, Kate, you tell me. I've got to go too, and I can't figure out why. It's supposed to be one of the perks of advertising—shooting on location."

"Well, Tangiers, *maybe* . . . Diamond Head, the Côte d'Azur . . . but Connecticut? I'm *from* Connecticut."

"Let me put it this way—if *I've* got to go, *you've* got to share my misery. Besides, you'll end up doing all sorts of interesting things to help out, and the place is really gorgeous. I'm trying to get Jess to book us at the Pequot Inn. It'll be fun." When Kate grunted skeptically, Esme demanded, "You got anything better planned?"

"Well, I'd go for a few days of solid sleep . . ."

"You get that between now and then—if you finish the paintings. Have you finished the paintings?"

Kate mused disgustedly, eyes skittering to her canvas and back. "I *will.*"

"You say that with a great deal of grit. What's the matter?"

"Nothing a nuclear war wouldn't clear up. Never mind. I'll finish the work. I'll be at the shoot. Just give me a little background on this place."

"It's not so much the place as the photographer. He's Joel Abbott."

"Hey, I *know* that name!"

"Of course you do. His book just came out—you know, the one about his trip to the prehistoric monuments in Wales. Well, he's a fashion photographer too—very successful and a close friend of Jess's. He's bought this old farm out in the Greenwich back country and turned the barn into a great big set—horizonless backdrops, the works. The Pequot Inn nearby is always featured in those travel magazines. It'll be pleasant—you wait."

"Sure. Good things come to those who wait. . . ." Kate muttered in resignation.

Esme's tired voice became crisp for a moment. "No, good things come to those who throw a net over them and haul 'em in."

Although she suspected that Esme's advice referred to more personal matters, Kate directed its message at her final, recalcitrant canvas.

It took her five days to finish it. She was ready to cry when she finally looked at the painting and saw neither gaping holes nor sludgy messes of careless color. The picture held together—it had depth and clarity, harmony, richness and drama. Evidently it wasn't necessary to enjoy the process of creation in order to come up with something worthwhile.

With weary relief Kate phoned the Exquisites

account group secretary and told her the final painting was ready to be sent off to the lab, which would make a huge backdrop from it.

Then she hung up her paint-encrusted apron and caught a subway downtown. She had a few days in which to fight some of the dust that furred her neglected apartment, to check in at her old haunts before her friends gave her up for dead and, most critical, to sleep.

The cleaning and sleeping palled quickly. She needed contact with the old crowd—her friends from art school and the drawing class she had taught, as well as those she'd hung out with at the galleries. Jeez, she thought, I could even see Ben! She wondered whether he was still her friend. She wondered whether she would really make the time to call him—she had only a couple of days.

Ben wandered into the Old Moscow Café late one afternoon. He had always favored it because of the pocket of obscure poets who had taken up residence in the middle room. Kate was reading an art magazine and eating a thick piece of brown bread layered with butter. Her hair was pulled back into a tight braid, and her black turtleneck covered her up to her jawbone.

"Well, you look like some ardent Russian revolutionary," he remarked. "All intense eyes and gaunt cheeks."

Startled, she looked up at his warm, mufflered face and experienced both a vague pleasure and a bit of dismay. He was a nice man, although he didn't arouse too much emotion in her. Maybe he was what she needed right now. She laid the magazine aside. "Won't you join me?"

"Yes, thank you."

"I was rather rude the last time I saw you," she said apologetically, dimly remembering the gallery opening.

"No, not rude so much as distracted. I had the impression you had something on your mind. The show, I guess."

"Yes. Well, it *was* rather a big event to get through," she said, remembering guiltily that what had distracted her from Ben had not been the show but Jess.

After coffee they took a leisurely stroll through the Village. Ben still had not taken up brisk exercise. They talked of new plays he had seen, city politics— in which he had an inexplicable interest—and of his upcoming trip to Athens. It was pleasant enough, although Kate occasionally felt she was in the first row of a lecture hall listening to a professor. What gave the evening most of its charm was the purity of the cool, autumnal air and the ever lively street life of Greenwich Village. They stopped and listened to a guitar player in Washington Square Park until Ben felt a chill. They munched on hot roasted chestnuts and read the reviews plastered on billboards outside of tiny playhouses. Near the New York University Law Library one of Ben's students hailed him and trotted over. He was an intense young man in jeans and a frayed army jacket. The falling temperature had put no color in his gaunt, anemic face, and his dark eyes burned with some fierce emotion. He attached himself to Ben, without even the barest nod to Kate, and launched into an urgent question about some assignments they'd had in class. Ben raised his eyebrows apologetically at Kate and answered. Soon the two had fallen into an utterly absorbed conversation. Kate let them walk on ahead of her, wondering if Ben would notice. He did not. She dropped further behind, her boots scuffing disconsolately over the brick walk. At another time she would have felt offended. She was smart enough to follow any of Ben's discussions, *and* add insights of her own, so he had no reason to exclude her, no excuse to be so rude. Jess would never have done so. The thought brought her up short. No good would come of letting her mind take such paths.

This time she found she had no emotion to spare to feel offended by Ben's neglect. She was just unhappy. The contrast between Ben and Jess was so glaring, so immeasurably vast, it could not easily be put into words. Ben courted her when it suited him, because he thought her exotic or interestingly arty, or for whatever other superficial reason. Jess put up with her because she was a critical part of his work. He could put up with anything when necessary.

And his kisses? Had *they* been necessary?

She looked around her in the failing light and did not see Ben or his student. They had lost her or she had lost them—it didn't matter. Breathing a short, bitter laugh into the dark, Kate pulled her coat around her and headed for home.

New York City seemed especially dreary with no painting blossoming on an easel. Kate always felt a little depressed when she was between projects. She usually combated the empty feeling by planning new projects or doing research for them.

She couldn't rely on the same method this time. In two days the Exquisites shoot would command her time and attention; she could not yet break herself free, exorcise the spirit of the jewelry project from her mind. She had merely to endure.

Esme had mentioned that she would like to go up to Greenwich the evening before the shoot—she said she could use an evening of rustic tranquility to get her thoughts in order. As the long morning of that last day wore on, Kate remembered Esme's comments gratefully. She picked up the phone.

"Oh, lordy," Esme groaned. "Don't even remind me that we start shooting tomorrow."

"But you're all on schedule with Exquisites, I thought."

"Exquisites, yes. It's those soda pop people who are ruining my life. They're terrified if I'm not around to hold their hands . . . their hand . . . oh, whatever. I hardly have time to go to the bathroom.

"Anyway, I'm spending the rest of the evening briefing my assistant so she can carry the torch for a few days. I'm not going to be free to get out to Connecticut early. Tomorrow morning, yes; tonight, no."

Kate sighed and tried to nudge away her disappointment.

Esme continued. "Hey, listen, no one says you have to wait for me. The room's already booked for us, after all. The Pequot is a gorgeous old inn—tiny but reeking with atmosphere—pewter plates on the walls, spittoons, hobnailed leather armchairs, the works. You go on up and absorb the ambience. Company's paying for it, so somebody ought to enjoy it."

"Will any of the others be there?"

"This early? Hardly. Though Felice and Michel left yesterday—I think they wanted a mini-vacation with one another. And Jess will be there to socialize with Joel and his wife Audrey, but he'll be staying at the house, so you won't see him."

Good, Kate remarked silently.

Most prominent among those who would not be there early was Genevieve Foucault.

After a bit of speculation, the idea of Greenwich and the tantalizingly described Pequot Inn began to appeal to Kate enormously. She threw together clothes that would lend themselves to assisting at a photo shoot in a barn and caught an evening train with the last of the rush-hour commuters.

The Greenwich railroad station and Greenwich proper admitted no hint of what lay beyond. The train station was functionally modern and melancholy in the way of all terminals on rainy nights. The town of Greenwich seemed composed of expensive colonial-style houses and tiny yards desperately crowded onto twisting, hilly roads. Interspersed were sudden clumps of sleek office buildings, all their windows dark, as they never would have been in Manhattan.

But as soon as the cab wended its way out of the downtown tangle, Kate found herself in the middle of woods as dense and luxuriant as they might have been in true Colonial days. She saw lights softened to wisps by the rain and fog and knew there were houses back behind the breaks in the trees. Once in a while a light at the side of the narrow, tortuously curved road would disclose shadows other than trees—stone walls, pillars, even cemeteries with worn, tilted headstones.

"Pequot's a nice place," the cabdriver offered loquaciously. Kate jumped, not used to friendliness in cabbies—or even cabbies who spoke English as their native tongue. If she hadn't known better she would have thought herself a lot further from Manhattan than that forty-five-minute train ride could have taken her.

"So I've heard," she replied enthusiastically.

"Hope you've got reservations. It's usually booked months in advance."

"Oh, yes—my company has made arrangements. We're in for a photography shoot." My company! She realized how readily the phrase now came to her lips.

"Ah," he responded. And said nothing further.

Not *so* different from Manhattan, Kate remarked to herself ironically, and she settled back to watch the white line uncurl down the ribbon of road.

Kate could see little of the Pequot Inn beyond its gray stone facade and the white door guarded by a fierce wrought-iron eagle on the lintel. Rain drove in sheets across the windshield, the cobbled driveway, and the awningless front stairs. Although the cabbie practically pulled onto the flagstone walk, she was well soaked by the time she hauled herself and her bag in through the main entrance. Her arrival set off a peal of little bells that cheered her and seemed to draw some of the chill from her bones.

The lobby looked like a movie set for an English gentleman's study. Prints of horses with their tails bobbed and nattily dressed squires lined the walls. Brass buckets—the spittoons, she guessed—held magazines and the day's papers. To the right, she saw a couple disappearing through a doorway. The muted sounds of clattering silverware and conversation told her that must be a dining room.

To the left lay a mammoth fieldstone fireplace laid with a generous, fragrant fire. Her damp body swayed toward it longingly, but she restrained herself; would have time for that after she had registered. The front desk was so well disguised by a polished walnut rail and inlaid green leather panels that it looked more like a piece of fine old library furniture than a focus of business. A balding head barely showed above the edge. She walked up to the desk, dripping rainwater, and looked over. The head belonged to a middle-aged man smoking a pipe and reading a paper as if the world had stopped flowing past him altogether.

"Good evening," Kate said softly.

He put down his paper, smiled around the stem of his pipe, and rose placidly. "Good evening. Quite a night out there. What can I do for you?"

"I'd like to check in. My name is Kate Angel."

The desk clerk frowned, as if seeking some elusive memory. "You were scheduled to arrive tonight?"

"Yes." Kate frowned also. Why didn't he check a list or something? Did he keep the entire schedule of the inn in his head? "I was booked for a double, but my friend won't be here until tomorrow. Perhaps you have it under her name—Esme Calladonna?"

"No . . . ah! With Mr. Schuyler's group?"

"Yes, that's it. You *do* have the reservation?"

"Yes—I have five rooms reserved for your party . . . starting tomorrow."

"Tomorrow! There has to be some mistake!" As the words left Kate's mouth she had the sickening feeling that the mistake had been Esme's . . . and hers.

"I'm terribly sorry, but Mr. LeClerc checked in today and verified that the five rooms would be needed starting tomorrow."

Mr. LeClerc, Kate mused. . . . "Can't you find something for me until then? I hate the thought of dragging all the way back to the city in this weather."

"I'm terribly sorry," he repeated. "We have only ten rooms. I'm afraid every one of them is filled. Why don't you let me make a few phone calls for you? One of the nicer motels downtown will have a vacancy. And it *will* be just for tonight."

Kate sagged against the velvet-smooth rail. "Well, I suppose I must. . . ."

The clerk gestured solicitously toward the snapping fire. "Please make yourself comfortable. You can leave your bag here."

Kate nodded and went to sit in a tall wing chair

that was angled toward the warming blaze. The strength had dribbled out of her body like grain out of a ripped sack. She had been very stupid to take Esme's word without checking. Poor Esme was so harried these days she could hardly be expected to remember such details. Still, it was a crummy way to begin what would doubtless be an ordeal to some degree anyway.

"Ms. Angel?" The desk clerk roused her. Kate trundled back to the desk and looked at the bit of writing he had put on a memo pad for her. "The Crystal House has a room for you. It's down on the water. Quite a nice place, really. I've taken the liberty of calling a cab for you."

"Thank you." She tried to seem appreciative but suspected that her words came out sounding pathetic. The big chair by the fire was a welcome refuge. She retreated there with a deep, weary sigh, already nostalgic for her rope chairs at home and her warm bed.

Her tiredness, the soothing fire, and the great lulling peace of the inn coaxed her into a half-doze until the lobby began to bustle in its muted way. Suspicious, Kate listened to the several voices coming from the regions behind her chair—they belonged to Felice, Michel and, yes indeed, Jess. She snuck a quick, furtive look around before diving back into the depths of the wing chair. The trio had apparently just come out of the dining room and were chatting amiably as they stood in the middle of a worn Oriental rug. The firelight caught the side of Jess's face, emphasizing the warm, intelligent look he had in daylight. He wore a casual suit of some dark color, but the usual smartly tailored shirt and beautiful tie had been replaced by a soft, creamy sweater. He looked almost Ivy League. As Kate hid in her corner by the fire, she wondered at her own taste. Her circle of friends, excepting musty old Ben, had always been style conscious, but on the funky side, as was supposedly appropriate for people in the arts. Seeing that look all the time had made her think that she preferred it, but Jess, in his serious, muted colors and classic styles, with the tiny, subtle accents of his jewelry, always looked good to her. She hoped this didn't signal a trend in her aesthetic.

A series of quiet good-byes and then silence told her that Felice and Michel had left the lobby. She heard Jess stop and say a few friendly words to the desk clerk. Now if he would only leave without coming near the fire . . .

With perfect bad timing, the desk clerk called, "Ms. Angel, your cab is here."

Kate momentarily squeezed her eyes shut in annoyance but gathered her things and stood up. There was no help for it now—Jess knew she was there. In fact, when she turned toward the desk he had already strolled halfway across the carpet toward her.

"Hi," she said inadequately. She felt uncomfortably small and juvenile, her clothing limp from the rain, her hair as wild as some urchin's. After she explained how she happened to be in her predicament, she would *truly* feel juvenile.

"Good evening," he replied pleasantly. Then a small frown crossed his softly highlit features. "You're leaving?"

She opened her mouth to explain in some way, but the desk clerk saved her. "I'm afraid we've made an error in Ms. Angel's reservation, Mr. Schuyler," he apologized untruthfully. "Her room will not be open until tomorrow, so I've taken the liberty of making arrangements at the Crystal House. I hope that is satisfactory?"

Jess's eyes had never left Kate, though he cocked

his head toward the desk to listen. "No, it isn't," he declared firmly. Then, more softly, to Kate he said, "There's no need for you to endure a motel—you can come back to Joel's house. He's got three extra bedrooms. . . . Uh uh! Before you begin one of your hard-nosed protests, let me finish—Joel and Audrey love company—they rattle around that big house like ghosts when they're alone. And second, you'll be handier for me there. . . ."

Kate's eyebrows threatened to rise right off her forehead, but Jess had not yet finished. "I would have had all my creative heads up at the house, but Felice and Michel have an idea of making this a vacation, and they want privacy. Esme is just antisocial. Maybe with you moved out of the inn we can coax her up to the house too. Then at least I'll have the two of you around if we need to work on problems after the day's shooting." He took a deep theatrical breath, smiled a little sheepishly, and said, "There, have I bowled you over with the force of my logic?"

"At least with the force of your nonsense. I'm a tired woman. I know I'll regret this when I'm coherent."

As Jess scooped her bag over his shoulder and touched his hand fleetingly to the small of her back to start her toward the door she knew she already regretted it.

The jilted cabdriver stood just inside the door. He had been listening to Jess's words as closely as had Kate, and he knew he had lost his fare. Before he could complain, Jess smiled, handed him a bill, and said, "For your trouble." Whatever the amount of the bill, it evidently recompensed the driver, for he tipped his hat at Jess and stepped aside. Kate had never seen anyone tip his hat before.

Jess took an umbrella from the bucket at the

entrance, opened the door, and thrust the huge black circle into the pounding rain. Kate slipped in underneath and squinted unsuccessfully through the sheets of water for a glimpse of the silver Jaguar.

"I'm parked over there," Jess informed her, seeming to read her mind. "The white car."

They headed for a dim shape parked along the circle of the driveway. Kate kept as much distance between them as she could, afraid that one more of his thoughtful little touches would make her do something unwise. In the lobby of the inn she had felt like a war orphan—homeless, dank, weary, and alone. And he had appeared providentially with the means to correct each of her troubles. She felt her defenses shaken. How could you dislike someone who saw to your comfort and well-being?

Jess looked at her sharply. "You're getting wet. Come here." He transferred the umbrella to his other hand and used his free arm to draw her more securely into its shelter. His arm slid into place along the curve of her waist, and his hand came to rest above the swell of her hip. He held her tightly enough to keep her from drifting off, yet softly, sensitive to the amount of freedom she needed to walk. She was quite comfortable . . . and very worried about it.

"Where's your coat?" she asked to distract herself.

"I left it in the car. I rarely feel the cold; I guess I'm very warm-blooded. Here we are."

He had led her to the passenger's side of a white Mercedes sedan. Kate jumped a little upon recognizing the make. He certainly had good taste in cars.

"You rack up the Jag?" she asked dryly.

"I thought I might be doing a little hauling for the shoot. A sports car isn't much good for that."

Whereas a Mercedes was perfectly suited for

hauling? Jess unlocked and opened the door and the subtle tobacco smell she had come to associate with him rolled out, warming the chill, damp night. Kate involuntarily looked up at him before stooping down to the seat. The casual smile had dissolved from his face, leaving it somber; his eyes were touched by thoughtfulness and caring. She wanted to pretend she hadn't seen his look, but Jess lightly touched her cold hand with his own warm fingers and said in a voice both tense and muted, "Kate . . ."

She turned away in confusion, muttering, "We're getting wet standing here."

No sooner had she pulled her legs and fingers inside the car than he slammed the door shut. The car rocked with the impact, and Kate pulled herself into a tight knot. She had made him angry again. Maybe he had only meant to ask her something harmless. . . . She felt a melancholy sense of déjà vu as he unlocked the opposite door and settled himself behind the wheel. It was bad to let things get so strained between them. Over the next few days she could hardly avoid him as she could have done at the agency. She *must* make an effort to act normally.

"Esme says your friend Joel is quite an eccentric," she said, uncertain whether that was a good start.

He didn't look at her as he chuckled, but at least it was an honest chuckle. "I wonder what Esme thinks *she* is."

"I'm sure she thinks she's hard working, serious, and businesslike."

"Well, one could argue that *that's* pretty eccentric. But yes, Joel's a character. And his wife Audrey is just as interesting. When you meet them you won't feel at all strange about staying at their house."

"You're very good friends then?"

He nodded, a gentle smile of reflection pushing

dimples into his cheeks. "I don't know if I like them *for* their quirks or in spite of them."

"You can't explain friendship in logical terms. You either feel it or you don't." She shut up, realizing what other emotion so defied logic.

Within a scant few minutes, Jess pulled into a crunchy gravel driveway lined with trees. His headlights briefly illuminated the eyes of two enormous wolflike creatures who bounded out of the way and followed alongside the car barking.

"Renaldoand Clara," Jess explained. "They're Russian wolfhounds. Don't judge them by their noise—they're a couple of milquetoasts."

The house came into view from behind a huge stand of lilac bushes. It was a compact pile of stone three stories high, trimmed with whitewashed wood, a slate roof, two chimney stacks, and a veranda that wrapped around two sides. Windows glowed here and there with light. Jess drove past. "The front entrance is grander, but the back door is sheltered."

He drove under a carport already inhabited by a jeep with a rollbar and a battered old Saab. Stacks of firewood lay against the wall of the house. Through the rain, before Jess turned off the headlights, Kate saw a lawn sweeping away to an irregular fringe of trees. The property must take up the space of a city block, she thought in awe.

She had jumped out of the car before Jess could come around to her side. The dogs concentrated on him, wuffling dementedly and wagging their tails so hard their big, bony hips swung back and forth. As soon as he had patted each and soothed them with a few affectionate words, they loped over to Kate. Aware that Jess was watching with curiosity, she calmly let them examine her and waited until they held up their heads to be scratched. In a few seconds they had decided she was acceptable and had dismissed her from their doggy minds.

"Well," Jess observed. "The city girl has a way with livestock."

She pouted. "I grew up in the wilds of eastern Connecticut, I'll have you know."

"Amid savage animals and dark, impenetrable forests."

"Absolutely. Well, it seemed that way to a kid. Actually, Manhattan is a lot wilder."

"Yes, it is. Come inside and get a taste of true civilization." He preceded her, carrying her bag.

With some trepidation, Kate followed. Despite his reassuring words, she felt awkward, like an intruder, in the house of people she didn't know. Her delight at the scene that met her eyes suspended her worry. The door led through a little foyer filled with boots and gardening tools and then into a vast kitchen. The floor was red brick, the cabinets were of weathered barn siding with rust-colored tiles paving the countertops. Bright bits of copper sparkled everywhere, and green plants trailed all over the calico-covered windows. A lime green picnic table supported the elbows of a thin woman in a flannel robe. Her red hair was softened with gray and swirled around her face like a mane.

"Coming in at all hours, I see." She grinned at Jess. Her voice was hoarse and too deep for her scraggly body. She included Kate in her warm regard before yelling at the dogs, "Get your flea-bitten noses out of here! Go out there and protect the property!" Renaldo and Clara promptly disappeared but, from the sloppy sounds of their play, Kate thought they were taking their responsibilities rather lightly.

"Audrey, this is Kate Angel," Jess informed her.

"Ah, yes, your artist. Well, come on in, honey. A

little dripping won't hurt this floor. You must be chilled to the bone. Jess Schuyler, did you leave her standing around in the rain? Look at her—she's *blue!* She's a very fetching blue, but she *is* blue." Audrey belted her worn robe more tightly and came over to peel Kate's coat off her.

"No, Audrey," Jess said defensively. "The damage had been done before I got to her. But I knew I could count on your gentle ministrations. Can we give her a room for the night?"

"We may even be able to scrape up a meal. How about it, Kate? I'll bet this sorry excuse for a man didn't feed you yet."

"Well . . ."

"Say no more, you're probably weak from his criminal neglect."

Kate had to smile at Audrey's scathing abuse. Jess, obviously used to such talk, put on a pathetically hurt look. "I'm only a man, Audrey. You've got to make allowances."

"Pshaw." Audrey really said "pshaw," but she said it as one who had only read it in a book and thought it pleasantly ridiculous. "The back bedroom is all made up. I'll take the poor thing up there now."

"I'll take her up," Jess said.

"No, you won't. You'll stay right here and call that Flip Trolley in New York."

"Trip Solley."

"Whatever. It's not a real name, after all. He sounded as though he were about to bust a seam when he called an hour ago. Why do you think I waited up so late? Just to make sure you called! Lord, it must be nine or ten o'clock."

Jess had reached for the white wall phone. "I'm dialing, I'm dialing!"

Audrey led Kate through a hallway papered above

the waist-high wainscot in an old, stenciled Victorian print. Modern photographs oddly mounted in antique frames peppered the walls. The floorboards creaked; the place smelled pleasantly musty and a little acrid—like photographic chemicals, Kate realized. The rooms she passed were cloaked in peace and darkness. She and Audrey clambered up one banistered stairway to another long hallway. Audrey took her to the end.

"There you go," she said heartily, turning on a light. "It'll warm up as soon as I bleed the radiator." She stalked over to an iron monster beneath a window with wooden sills and went to work. Kate looked around in amazement at the room. It had been whitewashed—walls, open-beamed ceiling, rough-boarded floors, and all—and the floor was covered in a pale blue rug. A big white four-poster bed sat snugly in the middle, piled with fat, blue-patterned quilts. There was a cushioned rocker beneath a good reading light and a big case of well-worn books.

"This is beautiful, Audrey."

Audrey smiled. "Thanks. Joel and I really don't have any use for such a big house, but I've enjoyed working on it."

"I can imagine you have. You can create a different little fantasy in every room. It's like painting."

"I suppose it is. There—the heat's coming on. Your bathroom is right next door; plenty of hangers in the closet, extra blankets in the hall closet. We passed the telephone on the landing—if you need it. Jess is in the room opposite this, and Joel and I are at the far end of the hall. We sleep like rocks," she added enigmatically. "Get yourself settled and come down for something to eat."

Chapter Nine

Kate did just that. She hung up all her clothes, peeled off the wet ones, and laid them over the radiator. Then she redressed in jeans and a huge red wool pullover. A good brushing almost dried her hair, but she left it loose so that it would be thoroughly dry by the time she went to bed. Then she padded downstairs in stocking feet. Just outside the kitchen she paused to listen to a deep male voice humming a familiar melody quite tunefully. Unnoticed she slipped into the kitchen. Audrey was nowhere to be seen. Jess was crouched down before the oven, staring through its glass window. He had discarded his jacket and had replaced his shoes with slippers.

"You really make yourself at home," she remarked, giving in to the half smile that tugged at her face.

"I have no other choice," he explained, rising. "If

I expected Audrey and Joel to wait on me I'd die of starvation. Speaking of which—can you handle chili this late at night? The larder around here tends toward food with a lot of personality. I can offer you cold sweet and sour pork, something that looks like half a Bavarian pancake, liverwurst . . ."

"Chili is fine!"

"Good, I'm already heating up the corn bread. Sit down."

"I can help . . ."

"No, no. I was stung to the quick by Audrey's accusations, and I insist on at least feeding you."

He seemed quite jolly about it, so Kate settled herself on one of the small benches around the green table and watched. Once again, Jess was showing her another side of himself. Certainly he would never give up his world of movers and shakers for the homey little world of brick-floored kitchens, but he seemed quite willing to enjoy it when it came his way. She watched his clean, graceful movements as he plucked two glasses from a shelf she couldn't have reached, then opened the refrigerator and frowned at its contents. "Milk? Beer? Fizzy red stuff?"

Bravely as she had accepted the offer of chili, she knew her stomach would need a little consideration. "Milk, please."

Jess whisked out the bottle, poured two glasses with a flourish, and set one on the table before her. He then set a red ceramic crock on the gas burner and found a wooden spoon in a drawer. The air was soon redolent with the spicy smell of chili.

"You seem to know your way around the kitchen pretty well."

"I lived with Joel and Audrey for a few weeks . . . after my divorce." His face had clouded. She was sure she saw deep lines etch themselves alongside his mouth as he turned his face away. So, the divorce still hurt him. Why? Because he didn't like to fail? To be found lacking? Because he still loved Genevieve? Such speculation disturbed her almost as much as the subject seemed to disturb him. She was relieved when he resumed a lighter tone of voice. "The lifestyle got into my blood. I keep thinking I'll buy a house someday, a bit of land for a yard and a garden . . ."

"Kids?" she asked without thinking.

He grinned teasingly. "Well, not by myself. I'm pretty talented, but there are some things I'll admit I can't do alone."

She tried to hide her blush by taking a swallow of milk and ended up choking. She waved away his help, managing to squeeze out the words, "Your chili's burning."

He rescued it as she recovered, dished out a bowl for her, and brought corn bread and butter. Then he sat down at the table to watch her eat.

"I want to be able to say I saw you leave the table alive, should anyone accuse me of trying to poison you with my cooking."

"I'm sure you know much subtler and slower ways of bumping someone off."

"A few." His eyes crinkled mischievously.

Being warm, fed, and sheltered and on such an easy level of joking with Jess made Kate happy. She could not, in her tiredness, regret feeling this way. "So what's on the agenda for tomorrow?" she asked with interest.

"We get up at the crack of dawn and go out to Joel's studio, or 'barn,' as we call it technically. The agency technicians came today and built the sets. Tomorrow everyone shows up—makeup, wardrobe, talent, gaffers, gofers, golfers . . . oops, I'm getting carried away."

"I get the feeling that Esme and I are really

extraneous—I mean, what do we *do* here while you're all working?"

"I hope you *will* be extraneous. That will mean everything is working out according to plan. It's only if something screws up that I'll need you to rethink the visuals. If everything goes well, just think of this as a gay romp through nature."

"It'll keep me healthy between visits to Central Park?"

"Exactly . . . Wait—you don't actually go into Central Park, do you?"

She laughed at his concern. "Of course I do. I get most of my exercise running from the muggers and the perverts."

He grinned ruefully. "I'm being heavy-handed again, aren't I?"

"A bit."

"Sorry. I'll try to keep myself in line. I do like it when things are pleasant between us."

She let herself meet his sincere dark eyes with a kind look. "I do too."

"Shall we be friends then?"

"Please." A sudden scrabble by the dogs at the doorway broke the mood and distracted them from any further agreements. Kate let Jess clear away the remnants of her meal and quickly bade him good-night, keenly aware of how well he seemed to know her, how close he had brought her to abandoning what prudence warned her to do. She hoped she would feel more like her tough, suspicious old self by the light of day.

By the light of day Kate felt raw with the beginnings of a cold. She dug vitamins out of the bottom of her bag and headed for the bathroom to take them before she forgot. The door to Jess's room stood open. The bed inside had been made and the curtains flung open to admit the brilliant morning sun. She hadn't made it up at the crack of dawn herself, but apparently Jess had. She poked her head through the doorway, called a tentative "Good morning," and then, reassured that no one was there, walked all the way in. Jess seemed to be able to live without clutter; she saw the edge of a suitcase stowed under the bed, a travel clock and several pairs of cufflinks on the night stand, a paperback biography of Winston Churchill opened over a pillow, and a pair of slippers warming by the radiator. That was it.

She went to the window and looked out over what proved to be a vast farmlotlike yard complete with a barn. A large truck shared the space in front of the barn with three vans. People traveled busily back and forth toting lights and crates. She picked Jess out right away—his cream white sweater caught the sunlight like a torch. He stood at the top of the bank on the barn's near side, gesturing to several people who held clipboards. He looked like the conductor of a great orchestra. The busy scene below made her feel an appreciation for the complexity of the shoot. She should hurry and try to be of some little help.

A quick shower woke her fully and washed away most of the symptoms of illness. She dressed in a flannel shirt over a sweater, jeans, and a quilted denim jacket. She braided her hair snugly out of the way and went to look for coffee.

That morning Audrey was running the kitchen. She was just handing a huge urn of coffee to an agency assistant when Kate tripped downstairs.

"Hi, hon," Audrey said in her surprisingly gravely voice. Kate wondered just how old Audrey was, to be calling her "hon" so comfortably. She didn't look more than forty-five. "I see you lived through the night."

"And slept like a log! I didn't hear any of the trucks pull in or the work get started. Have all these people been here for hours?"

"A couple of hours. Nothing important's started yet, though—just a lot of yelling and arguing about where to put things. Here, sit down and stoke your furnace. I've got corn bread, if you're not sick of it, apples, cheese . . ."

"Stop right there. If you can siphon a cup of coffee out of one of those urns for me that'll be perfect."

As Audrey obliged, Kate reached for a square of warm, crusty corn bread that lay in a cloth-lined basket. This must be Audrey's specialty, Kate thought, taking a hungry bite. And a wonderful one to have. Mug in one hand, bread in the other, she quit the house for the lively backyard.

Jess's white Mercedes gleamed in the shade of the carport. The old Saab was just as decrepit as it had looked the previous night. The jeep was gone. She squeezed around the two cars and struck out across the soft ground. The smell of damp leaves and car exhaust made an odd perfume.

The first sight that caught her attention was that of Esme sitting on a felled tree trunk, looking odd, if not totally out of place, in her black leather pants and big-shouldered purple jacket. She had exchanged her usual spike heels for flats, but they were thin soled and unequal to the terrain.

She squinted as Kate joined her; she was not much used to sunlight. "Morning. You look insultingly chipper."

"*You* look like someone dragged you out of your burrow."

"Thanks. Actually, that's better than I feel. Sorry about my mistake over the reservation."

"No problem. One soft bed is as good as another. Where's Jess?"

"Piloting the ship from . . . oops, no. He's gone. Well, he moves faster than a Times Square pickpocket. *We* should have such purpose in life."

"Why *are* we here, Esme?"

"Beats me. Want to run away?"

A man spoke ominously from behind them. "I'd hunt you to the ends of the earth."

Kate swiveled around and looked up into the handsome face of her boss. His cheeks glowed and his eyes shone brown as a polished tiger's eye. His long, muscular legs and lean hips looked a lot better in jeans than those of most men Kate's age. Bits of gold-and-red leaves stuck to his cable-knit sweater. Kate resisted the urge to reach up and pluck them off. Instead, she simply reached up and let him raise her to her feet in one sure pull. She grinned irrepressibly, delighted with the way he seemed to sparkle in the fresh, rarified sunlight. He looked elementally alive, a warm, exuberant animal.

"You'd better give us something to do, or we might just wander off," she said teasingly.

"I'll give you a little tour and then load you with responsibilities. Coming, Esme?"

"Thanks, but I'll just sit here and let my responsibilities find *me*."

As naturally as the wind rustled the leaves, Jess took Kate's hand and helped her over the log. His touch was light and lasted only until she had hopped to the other side, but she felt she had somehow connected with a power source. Her fingers tingled, her awareness of him and her surroundings changed and heightened. She also felt suddenly self-conscious, as if the strength of her feeling must have broadcast itself to everyone. That was ridiculous, of course, but still she looked around surreptitiously, waiting for funny looks. She got none—just a few of passing curiosity from people she didn't know.

Jess led her into the barn, the focus of all the activity. Joel had turned it into a dry, well-heated photo studio. Its only barnlike survival was the high, open-beamed ceiling, and even that had been permanently altered by festoons of lights and cables. She and Jess had approached the actual shooting area from the back. Jess picked his way over equipment and she followed carefully as they made their way around. She looked up from watching her footsteps only when she noticed Jess himself stop. He motioned her to turn her attention to the main space.

She gasped. There stood a fifteen-foot-high backdrop made from her first painting. The sight was unnerving. It was also, she realized, beautiful. The shapes sliced across the space with power and energy. The colors were true—rich, yet subtle. Blown up to that incredible size, the image looked even better.

Jess allowed her a few moments to exult and then asked in a quiet voice, "Was it worth it?"

She got control of the idiot grin that threatened to split her face and cocked her head slyly. "The beauty is, of course, due to me, but the pretentiousness can only be yours."

"Touché!" he laughed. "Although in advertising we call it conviction."

A peal of notes from a car horn brought up the heads of everyone in the barn. Jess frowned comically, rolling his eyes, and said, "It must be Joel, or someone he's training to be flamboyant. Come on, you've got to meet him sometime."

Eager for her first glimpse of Jess's eccentric friend, Kate trotted away from her backdrop and out into the sunshine. The missing jeep had left skid marks over the mud around the parked vehicles; its inhabitants seemed to be cowering from the ride— all but the driver. He leaped heedlessly to the ground, sighted Jess with eyes of keen blue, and called in a voice to match Audrey's, "Hey, you still here? I thought I told you gypsies to clear off my land by sunup."

Joel was Jess's age or a bit older, but his wild hair had gone a grizzled gray that almost matched his incredibly faded denim jacket and jeans. He had a full beard and mustache that bristled out like steel wool, and he walked with an exaggerated cowboy slouch. His air of total ease and friendliness made Kate like him instantly.

"Hey, Jess," he continued. "Look what I brought you."

At that Kate's morning dimmed. Climbing out of the jeep were the Exquisites models—most particularly, Genevieve Foucault. The blonde had waited pointedly for someone to help her down from the high-seated car but, when it became apparent that no one was going to do so, she gracefully lowered herself to the ground, wincing as her small, suede-shod feet touched the mud. She pulled her fox jacket tightly around her shoulders and stared accusingly at Jess. He had paled to an unhealthy color, and seemed to have lost the exuberance that had buoyed him all morning.

Kate willed him to stay away from the woman, applying her mind with a passion that came from unexplored depths, but Jess walked forward a few steps anyway. Genevieve babbled some pretty words in French, her tone insufferably intimate. Kate wished she could remember some of her high school French, though doubtless it would have done her little good—Genevieve's accent was too fluid, too gracefully slurred.

Jess answered, equally fluent but gruff. Genevieve pouted, trilled another coaxing sentence and put out a white-gloved hand. Jess, oblivious to the cursing he

was getting from Kate's heart, let the delicate hand
rest upon his arm and led Genevieve toward the
barn.

It took hours before Kate could make herself go
back to the photo studio. She kept busy by helping
the technicians and miscellaneous hands outside—
running down lost items, making phone calls, fetching coffee. She told herself she was earning her pay
more that way than by sitting inside watching Joel do
his work. Esme periodically popped out and re-
ported that things were going all right. Not
splendidly—she wouldn't say that, but she wouldn't
elaborate.

Kate would have occupied herself with trivia all
day except that Michel and Felice showed up before
lunch. They looked relaxed and happy with each
other—apparently the "mini-vacation" was agreeing
with them. Kate thought back on what Felice had
said about tolerating Michel's little flirtations. Obviously she wasn't as hard shelled as she had claimed.
It seemed quite clear that Felice had offered her
playboy some options and they were both now
enjoying his choice. Kate had to be glad for them—
if, at the same time, she felt a little melancholy.

"Ma chère!" Felice called in her silvery voice. She
wore an amazingly blousy khaki jumpsuit flowing
with scarves at the neck. She even wore a pith
helmet.

"What is this, Felice? The Foreign Legion?" Kate
teased.

"Oh, when do I get to act dashing and romantic in
New York? Today I am on safari in Connecticut,
stalking big game." Her eyes glittered as she looked
theatrically toward Michel, who was himself impos-
ing in a khaki safari suit.

"Felice, I think you've already bagged your big
game."

"Oh, don't let him know! He so loves the chase! Listen, petite, you must fill me in on all we have missed—we spent so much time getting up this morning . . ."

"I'm sorry, Felice, I haven't been in on the shoot, really. They're kind of crowded in there and so I thought . . ."

Felice glared sternly. "Crowded, nonsense! You are a *chicken*, that's what I say. Come with me, *enfante*." She grasped Kate's wrist in a powerful, thin-fingered grip and dragged her to the barn.

The barn was indeed crowded—a scene of marvellously ordered confusion. It took Kate a few moments to locate the principals: two models, Sandy and Greta, posed before the backdrop; Joel swung around them taking pictures as fast as his whirring autodrive would let him. Jess watched from the sidelines and, of course, Genevieve stood with her hand negligently dangling against Jess's arm. When Joel called for her to join the other two, Jess looked up at her, gave her an unnervingly sweet smile and squeezed her hand encouragingly. She swept out to the spotlit patch of floor with the assurance of a queen. Her pale blond hair had been pinned up in a gleaming chignon, the backless pumpkin-colored silk dress floated liquidly over her long, elegant body. She wore one of Kate's favorite necklaces—an amber and jet choker that trailed a long strand of beads from the gold clasp. It dangled provocatively over the pearly skin of her back. The other girls looked good—flawless jewels in their own right—but Genevieve had an added allure, a bold sensuality that Kate knew was for Jess's benefit. She wanted to turn away in disgust but morbid curiosity made her stay.

Jess watched his ex-wife, a critical frown poised lightly over his features. Every time Genevieve sent him a smile or a coy look, which Kate thought exaggeratedly often, he smiled back. They had been through this many times, Kate realized. Jess had once been accustomed to watching his beautiful wife twirl and posture before a camera. What did it bring to his mind now? Happy memories? Regret for past mistakes? Kate tried not to speculate. He looked too comfortable back in his old role.

He didn't have to look so darn approving! Kate came close to stamping her foot, but she held herself to a tightening of her lips. Genevieve was transparently playing up to him, flirting with him, reminding him of the intimacies they had shared. Why, the woman still seemed to regard him as her possession —and he was allowing her! Kate growled silently and left to breathe some less potent air outside.

Out in front of the house a couple of agency employees were playing, or trying to play, Frisbee with the wolfhounds. Kate sat on the steps of the veranda and watched, her thoughts glum. She had let herself get too involved with Jess. Their lack of any real relationship mattered not at all—she was in love with him, and watching him with his ex-wife was torture. Watching him in any circumstances was torture. Her original decision to stay clear of him still held, if only her emotions would obey. Anyone who could have this strong an effect on her over the distance she had put between them was dangerous. She no longer needed Andrew around to grind her face in that truth. How she longed for her old independence! The days when she could paint through the night without someone making remarks seemed like bliss.

"Watching Frisbee is hungry work," Jess said behind her.

She turned involuntarily and saw him in the doorway holding open both the main door and the

storm door. From the shadowed interior of the
house came a ripple of bell-toned words, this time in
English but unmistakably Genevieve's. "Come,
Jess, you are letting the heat out and I am wearing
only this scrap of a dress."

Jess glanced at the speaker, made some pleasant
reply that Kate could not catch, and turned back to
her. "How about it? We've sent out for fried
chicken."

"No, thanks," she said dully. "You *are* letting all
the heat out, you know."

She didn't have to see his face to know the hard
expression he wore as he let the storm door slam.
The sound went through her like a bomb blast, but
she sat tight, knees drawn up, arms wrapped around
her legs, chin lowered in misery.

Kate hid for the rest of the day. After making sure
that Jess intended to eat elsewhere, she met Esme
for dinner at the Pequot. They exchanged a few
comments about the next day's schedule but Esme
was tired and Kate was depressed. Their years of
friendship let them eat in companionable silence.

Back at Joel and Audrey's house later that night
she tossed restlessly in the big four-poster, listening
to the sounds of activity outside die away. Funny, it
hadn't occurred to her to move back to the Pequot,
to the room booked for Esme and her. Better for
Esme—at least one of them would sleep.

Finally the urge to prowl overwhelmed her, so she
threw on a robe and opened the door to the darkened hallway—and stopped. A light gleamed softly
in Jess's room, showing him standing at the foot of
his own bed, bent forward with his arms braced on
the rail of the footboard. His shirt was off, and the
warm light from the night lamp washed gold over the
powerful lines of his body. His back and ribs were

sheathed by taut, fluid muscles; his arms swelled with strength. She could see the blur of soft black hair that began in the hollow at the base of his throat, trailed provocatively over his flat stomach, and disappeared beneath his belt. Then he shifted and, apart from being mesmerized by the graceful flow of his muscles, Kate now noticed shapes on the bed. He was looking at photos—proofs of the day's shooting.

She thought better of stepping onto the creaky old hall floor. Instead, she quietly stepped back into her own room and shut the door.

The next morning Kate and Esme were able to pore over the proofs themselves and so keep occupied. They turned a parlor next to the kitchen into a workroom. Joel did exceptional work; he clearly deserved his reputation. His photos, even these, taken on a set that was nothing more than a backdrop with models in front of it, had a feeling of clean, soaring space and brilliant light. Her painting looked like stained glass.

"Oh, this is yummy," Esme crowed. "I *live* for this." She had completely recovered from her exhaustion of the past couple of weeks.

"You mean you don't do this for the sake of the late nights, the bad cafeteria food, and the presentations to idiot clients?"

"Well, there are *those* attractions too. . . . Look at this one, Kate—the color, the vibrance, the way the lines of her legs and arms focus your eye toward the brooch. It doesn't even need to be trimmed. Oh, this is going to be fun!"

They worked at marking the negatives to be rough printed, matching them to various layouts that had been formatted at the agency. Kate began to see clearly the final look of the ads, and she realized how good Jess's concept had been.

"They're going to work, Esme!" she breathed in wonder.

Esme cackled, "They sure are!"

About mid-afternoon, they heard a commotion outside on the still damp driveway. Men yelled, a horn squawked obnoxiously and, after a minute or two, a woman's voice screeched—in French. Esme jumped to the window.

"Oh, my God!" she exclaimed and dashed for the door as fast as her unexercised legs could take her. Kate speared her pencil through her hair and followed hastily. Anything that upset Esme had to be serious.

A dark blue Citroën sat at an erratic angle in the driveway, its front bumper a finger's width away from the side of a paneled van. Enough arguing people had gathered to raise a din that could be heard all the way back to Manhattan. Loudest of all, because of her shrillness, was Genevieve. She wore the white tuxedo-jacketed gown scheduled for that afternoon's photo session, and her elaborately coiffed hair was falling from its pins because of her agitation. She was directing all her fury toward the driver of the Citroën—a pale young man with laboriously styled brown hair and sleek, expensive clothes. Kate caught his name as Genevieve venomously spat it out—Philippe. So this was the notorious gambling Philippe, the man who had Genevieve so tangled in his unsavory affairs that she had come scurrying back to Jess! He looked lightweight and feral; Kate couldn't see his appeal.

Jess, on the other hand, looked the very epitome of stern strength. He had arrived on the scene from

the direction of the barn and closed in until he was at
Genevieve's side, undemonstrative but alert and
poised. His call to action came in a sequence of
exchanges between Genevieve and Phillippe that
were straight from a movie: Philippe asked a question in a scornful voice; Genevieve declined acidly
and spat at his feet; he roared, grabbed her wrist,
and tried to yank her into the car; she shrieked. Jess,
a black fury suffusing his face, took Philippe's of-
fending arm in a grip so viselike that, even after the
gambler had been forced to free Genevieve, his
fingers remained splayed open in pain. Finally Jess
released him with a jerk. He then backed the
shocked young man into his car and, in English and
French, if not in several other languages as well,
ordered him off the property. Philippe needed no
further convincing. The blue car squealed in reverse
all the way down the drive.

Genevieve stood with her long, graceful hands
fluttering tremulously over her face; her shoulders
shook with the delicate force of her crying. Even
Kate suspended her suspicions in favor of sympathy
for the woman. Whatever Philippe's crimes, they
certainly upset Genevieve. Why did Jess look so
angry? His lips were pulled tight across his teeth,
holding back the words he obviously wanted to say.
He offered Genevieve neither a kind word nor
touch. Kate was confused, not the least by her own
sudden sympathy for the blonde. Jess had just driven
off her tormentor, in true knightly fashion, yet now
he showed no trace of compassion for the suffering
woman.

Genevieve sobbed audibly and Kate, despite her
own pity, wondered anxiously if makeup could hide
the effects. She had an uncomfortably vivid sense of
the irreplaceable minutes of shooting time speeding

by. How callous I've become, Kate thought in surprise. No, her cynical inner voice countered, you have always been this way—nothing should interfere with work, with obligations. If you chose a path you stuck to it. She was just like Jess—each was hard as flint on this subject. No wonder such sparks flew when they were together.

Everyone still standing near the scene showed the same apprehension. They couldn't drift off to their work—there really was no work until Genevieve herself resumed it, and Genevieve had lowered her hands in order to lavish Jess with a look from her suffering, though oddly dry, eyes.

His voice was quiet, but the dead silence made it audible. "Why don't you go up to the house for a while? We'll wait for you." It seemed a good suggestion, and generous, in view of their tight schedule.

Kate watched as comprehension spread a white-hot pallor across Genevieve's ivory skin, and then, high on each cold cheek, a patch of red flamed. Her eyes looked fevered—and angry.

"You expect me to *work* after this?" Her voice carried a snappish obstinacy quite at odds with her wounded pose.

The muscles in Jess's jaw bunched tightly; his reply barely squeezed out through his clenched teeth, but it came out sounding carefully reasonable. "Yes, Genevieve, I do. The shooting is planned around you. We *need* you to work."

A cunning smile slipped into her thinning mouth. Outrage was totally wiped off her face by a look of calculation. Kate's mouth opened in a weak gasp— the woman wasn't upset at all, she was *manipulative*. She hadn't been able to capture Jess's sympathy, so she thought now to pressure him. "Certainly I can't be that important. There are so many other pretty girls in New York. Surely you won't notice if I am missing for a few hours—just long enough to restore myself . . ."

"We can't afford a few hours. You know how close we are to deadline."

"Oh deadline, deadline!" she said lightly. "Don't you ever consider anything other than business?"

Jess replied in a tight voice, "We are here for business. And only business. What are *you* here for?"

Kate jumped. She hadn't expected him to be so bald about it. She hadn't actually considered how clearly Jess himself might see through his ex-wife. Genevieve had been knocked subtly off balance, her aplomb damaged.

"Well, I see you cannot truly be so concerned for your precious photo shoot if you find such pleasure in baiting me when I am already upset. A little kindness, perhaps . . ."

His quiet voice dropped to new softness. Kate shifted miserably, wishing her cold had hung on and rendered her hard of hearing. "I spent too many years coaxing you against your nature, Gen. It's not worthwhile."

She stamped her foot resoundingly on the ground, surprising everyone with the force produced by one of such delicate appearance. "Not worthwhile?" she demanded loudly. "I am quite nicely put in my place! I leave you then, to discover better uses for your precious time and energy."

Then she did indeed walk off.

Chapter Ten

Kate never learned exactly how Genevieve's exit was made because she herself had fled determinedly to the house, appalled at the prospect of meeting Jess's eyes and acknowledging that she had witnessed the whole wretched scene.

Esme found her later halfheartedly reading the titles of the books in her bedroom.

"Come on, Kate. Powwow downstairs."

"Has Genevieve left?"

"Oooh boy," Esme answered, rolling her eyes. "Has she ever! And made a mess of our schedule."

Downstairs in the little room off the kitchen Jess, Felice, and Joel pored over proofs and layouts. Jess had a telephone squeezed between ear and shoulder, and his hands were full of clipboards. He glanced up when Kate entered. "You're about to find out why I needed you along for the shoot, Kate."

She shrugged and answered as lightly as she could, "At least I'm earning my pay." The party on the other end reengaged Jess's attention. She went to look over Felice's shoulder, and by the time Jess had finished the call and started the next, she was caught up in the work.

Genevieve's departure had left a hole in their plans. Jewelry, clothing, models, and backdrops had been carefully matched to show all to best advantage. Without Genevieve, or without a blonde with her basic qualifications, each item had to be reshuffled, the combinations reworked and tried against the overall scheme of the campaign. That was their *worst* contingency—working without a third model. Jess was on the phone trying to locate the few models he had considered before Michel had saddled them with Genevieve. Meanwhile, should his efforts fail, Kate and her fellows struggled with a salvage plan.

Periodically he checked with them on particular points.

"Dana Quinn is available, but she's a size smaller than Gen."

Esme fetched the head dresser and discussed pinning the clothes tighter. "No can do, Jess. Everything left is slinky or fitted. Could have done it with the blousy stuff, but . . ."

And Jess returned to the phone.

"Tiara Stewart," he suggested later. "I don't really remember her, but her agency says she's a strawberry blonde."

Felice frowned. "They're liars. Her hair's as red as Kate's is black."

And so on.

Kate wondered whether a computer would have been useful in the rescheduling. There were so many factors! Every time she thought of something that seemed feasible, someone would remember a detail that threw the whole thing awry. How had they figured it all out in the first place? Everything had been flexible then—models and clothes. Now half the shoot was down on film, and time was galloping forward.

Impossible as it seemed, they finished. It surprised them all.

"Incredible!" Esme mumbled through her nail-bitten fingers. "We've run out of pieces of jewelry."

"Nah," Joel said in disagreement. "What about that little jingly thing with the pearls?"

"That's in group four—with Greta in the blue scoop neck."

"Oh, yeah. . . . The brooches that all look like pineapples?"

"Group seven."

"The chokers . . ."

"No, Joel! Come on, give it up! We've *finished*. And it's only . . . oh, jeez, two-thirty in the morning."

Esme might have been surprised at the time, but Kate felt every laborious minute like a weight upon her head. She believed it was two-thirty in the morning, but she couldn't have said of *what* morning. Joel had drunk beer all night long without losing any of his acuity or quirky humor. Coffee was making her hands shake and her stomach turn in on itself, so Kate had unwisely decided to drink a bottle herself. It had been the last nudge toward exhaustion. She wondered whether Audrey would mind if she crawled under the table and slept there.

Jess had the decency to look slightly fatigued, though he had flagged the least of all of them. His thick hair lay in ruffled waves from the passage of his fingers, his eyes held slight shadows, but he looked very little worse than he had during the strain of the afternoon. Perhaps that had been the worst for him. After all, he *throve* on work. Still, it wasn't fair that he should look so together when Kate felt totally limp.

She realized that in her weariness she had mumbled this last observation aloud. Jess raised one eyebrow at her. He shook his head in bemusement. "What's not fair? I hope you don't want to get into a philosophical discussion this late at night. I can hardly remember my own name."

She dragged her chin off the table. "The only thing I want to get into is a big, soft bed."

"Go! Go!" he ordered severely. "We're all set for tomorrow whether Caroline Hite can make it or not. Blonde or no blonde, we're covered. But go to bed before you die on me—a consultant is even harder to replace than a model."

"Right, boss," she agreed in a happy slur. She picked herself up and managed a good imitation of walking until she took a wrong turn into the dark, deserted living room. The distance across to the door into the main hallway was too great to be contemplated and was cluttered with treacherous furniture that reached out to knock her tired shins. What did she need a bed for anyway? The couch there was soft. It would do nicely. . . .

So Jess found her a few minutes later, already so solidly asleep on the couch she didn't wake when he turned on a light. Her face had lost all its toughness, all the sternness she forced upon it, and had relaxed into sweet, pretty lines. One hand clutched a little square pillow against her chest as if she needed something to cuddle. Her lashes lay thick and motionless on her smooth cheeks, and her lips looked as soft as rose petals. Looking down at her, lost in wonder and regret, Jess longed so badly to kiss her that he unconsciously began to kneel down. He caught himself in time. Tiredness was no excuse. Awake, she would not want his kiss; he could not force it on her asleep.

Still unwilling to tear himself away, he knelt again on the floor and felt the room's coldness seep into his knees. She'd freeze down here. She probably wasn't as indestructible as she seemed to think, although he thought proudly how well she did always seem to hold up. A blanket? he wondered. No, a blanket wouldn't be enough. She needed a bed, with thick quilts tucked around her.

He allowed himself very little, so when he did slip his arms around her and pick her up, it was with mixed feelings of pleasure and guilt. It was all very well to tell himself he was merely being kind and looking out for her welfare, but his conscience told him otherwise. He liked to feel her in his arms. She felt warm and sturdy. Even in sleep her healthy muscles kept their firmness, their silky weight. He could feel her heart beating next to his, her breath gently sweeping his neck. When she sighed unexpectedly and curled her hand around a fold of his sweater the same way she had held the pillow, his heart nearly stopped.

He stood looking down at her mysteriously shadowed face and knew he had made a mistake by ever touching her—not just this time, but that very first, when he had kissed her "for luck" at the presentation and felt a surge of power and longing in his veins that had never subsided. There was no help for it. He could only tuck her into her bed and steal away, hoping she would never find out how she got there.

Jess's intentions were very good. He got her to the bed, laid her down, pulled off her shoes, and pulled the covers over her. Things got more complicated after that. In the uncertain light filtering through the window from the half moon, it was hard to see anything, but he thought for a moment that she had opened her eyes and seen him there. He was never sure. He *was* sure, however, when she reached up softly with both hands and pulled his face down to hers. Her lips were shy but warm. Unable to locate his better judgment, he kissed her tenderly, spellbound by a longing he had been afraid to acknowledge. Her lips opened like a blossom, tantalizing his mouth with sweetness. His teeth played gently over their soft contours and his hunger for her grew until he could no longer be satisfied with so slight a contact. He drew back.

Then he knew she was really asleep. Had she been awake and wanted him, she would have given some sign—a little cry, the pressure of her hands on the back of her neck, *something*. But she merely snuggled deeper into the feather pillow, a tiny smile curved upon those bewitching lips.

Impossible regret filled him as he pulled himself away from her side. Staying with her could accomplish nothing beyond entrenching his own pain. What he had told Genevieve applied to Kate, though the two were as different as acid and balm. He did not coax women to act against their natures. Kate was rational, adult, and extremely strong-willed. If she had chosen him willingly, those qualities would have forever been a source of joy and pride to him. Without them she would have been a different Kate—weak, simpering, foolish. He couldn't regret the way she was made, only that Andrew Keene had poisoned her toward *him*.

He softly stole from the room and left her deep in her dreams.

Kate's dreams held her tenaciously until the clamor of someone in the hall dragged her awake. She looked blearily around the room with an inexplicable smile on her face, even though her head was muzzy and leaden. A sense of urgency propelled her out of the bed before she had a chance to recapture the details of the last pleasant dream. Such lazing around was not for someone finishing up a shoot. She finally felt connected with the work. Jess really hadn't invited her along gratuitously. The night before she had truly earned her pay, whether or not the new model showed up today. This knowledge put a certain lift into her step that disguised her tiredness.

She made a much better appearance than Felice and Esme, whom she found in the kitchen, puffy eyed and yawning.

"Good morning," she said brightly to their grouchy faces. "Is Caroline Hite coming?"

Felice nodded. "Yes; we must have the favor of the gods—it is raining in Vermont on the site of her current job, and so she comes to us."

"Then we can go ahead with the original schedule?"

Esme groaned. "Yes. All that gruelling work for nothing. We have our blonde. I sure hope she's the last one we have to deal with on this job. How Jess can deal with her so equably I can't imagine."

Kate heartily and silently agreed. If she ever learned to deal thus with Andrew, she would be much the better for it. This thought sobered her as she poured coffee and fried herself an egg in the skillet.

While she was engaged in crunching a piece of toast and butter, Jess came in to get Felice's opinion on something. He had been up before anyone, organizing the crew, filling Caroline in on the job. He finally looked tired, so tired that Kate paused to consider her own warm flush of blood at the sight of him. Then she remembered her dreams—even though she had stayed so determinedly clear of him in her waking life, in sleep she had lain in his arms, making luxurious, wanton love with him. The memory of it shocked her, and one look at him brought back the details—the feel of his strong hands stroking her, the smell of his hair and skin, the taste of his tongue in her mouth, salty from its exploration of her own flesh. A shudder passed through her as she remembered; silly of course—no one could control their dreams—it was your waking behavior you had to watch.

Then Jess's eyes caught hers for a fraction of a second and slid away. He couldn't! He couldn't know! But Kate had a vivid, terrifying impression that he somehow knew exactly what had been in her mind. Why else would he have looked at her with such particular intensity and then looked away, as if he were embarrassed by what he saw?

It was *absurd*. She told herself that firmly and tried to attend to her food. Jess hung around the coffee urn, though his business with Felice seemed to be done. He stood stirring his coffee round and round, which made no sense to Kate, since she knew he took it black. He had nothing to say to anyone and would not look up. Kate's tension throttled her so that eating became impossible. Why didn't he leave? Why didn't he say something?

"Did you have a good night, Kate?"

She dropped her fork. Felice had wandered out to the carport, but Esme cast her a sharp look from the opposite chair. Thank God Jess could not have seen it. Something was wrong, or there was something going on that she didn't understand. She casually tapped the crumbs off a piece of toast and replied, "Fine."

His eyes lingered on her longer than was necessary

and then dropped. "Good . . . I'm afraid yesterday's strain was a bit much." It sounded lame.

"Well, as long as we get through today all right . . ."

"I suppose so."

What an impossible conversation! Kate didn't need to see Esme's suspicious expression to know how stilted it sounded. She wished he would leave so she *could* get through this day. Abruptly Jess set his mug in the sink with a nerve-jarring clatter and left.

Esme waited until she heard his footsteps sound on the flagstone walk that led to the driveway. Then, her dry voice unusually full of feeling, she asked, "What happened with you two last night?"

"Nothing!" Kate insisted sharply. "What do you mean 'what happened'? I went to bed and slept like a log. Why do you think something *happened?*"

"Sorry! Just wondering why you looked so green when he asked you how your night went. Calm down, will you? It's none of my business what's going on between you two."

"Exactly. Especially since there's *nothing* going on." Kate found her eyes had widened in a challenging glare. Unfortunately, a lighter tone was completely beyond her, so she merely attacked her food and let Esme examine the top of her head.

"When are you taking off today?" the blonde asked, trying a more diplomatic vein.

"How long are we expected to stay?"

"Well, not to the bitter end, but at least until Joel calls it quits. Jess will stay until the sets are struck, probably longer actually, but that's his cross to bear. I'm catching a ride with the first likely looking person. You?"

"I guess I'll do that too. Or take the train . . ."

"Will you be relieved to get away from this advertising stuff and back to your loft?"

"You don't know the half of it!" Kate replied, hoping Esme *didn't* know.

It turned out to be an extremely dull day. Everyone involved with the actual shooting worked diligently to make up for lost time, and so no one was around to keep Kate amused. She packed her bag for the return trip to Manhattan and looked again at the marked proofs lying scattered over the table in the workroom. She was useless again, bound by an unspoken but formal obligation to see the day through. Oh, she *would* be so relieved to get back to the world she knew, the world she had made for herself in Manhattan. Relieved, certainly; maybe not exactly happy.

Shooting continued through lunch, so Kate took a sandwich and a glass of cider and wandered aimlessly into the trees on the far edge of the property. Just where the property ended, Kate could not tell. The trees thickened into a respectable tangle of woods and spread lazily over uninterrupted hills and gulleys. She did not fancy herself a frontiersman and kept close enough to hear the sounds coming from the shoot. Just past the rise of a hill she discovered a flat slab of New England granite angled gently toward the afternoon sun. Its surface felt as warm as a living body, and Kate spread herself upon it like a cat. With food in her stomach, the warmth of the sun and her unallayed tiredness quickly sent her into a drowse. It was as good a way as any to spend these last few hours, she thought. No one would miss her.

The chill woke her; that and the crunch of steps on the few newly fallen dry leaves. She scooped herself off the rock with unexpected vigor, thankful her mind had awakened as quickly as her body. The producer of the footsteps was not a mugger or a bear, it turned out, but Jess—who might, she realized, be more dangerous. As she dusted herself off and arranged her clothes, he came around a tree trunk, a scowl darkening his face. She knew what the scowl was for.

"I've been looking all over for you," he announced in annoyance.

"What are you? The Royal Canadian Mounted Police? No, I guess not—you would have found me before this. I must be all of four hundred feet from the edge of the lawn," she snapped.

"Far enough away to get lost."

"No, Jess, just far enough away for *you* to lose *me*." With an angry toss of her braid, she struck off past him. She didn't allow a wide enough berth, for he reached out and grabbed her wrist. Off balance, she barely managed to catch herself before she squared her shoulders and stood there glaring at him. The expression on his face confused her. It was so sad, so unsure.

"That's just what I'm trying not to do, Kate—lose you."

"What? Let go of my arm!"

"No." He refused adamantly and took hold of the other one as well. Now they were face to face, so close she could see every bloodshot streak in his tired eyes. "You're too stubborn, Kate. I won't let you ruin both of our lives."

"Stop talking nonsense. Now that this project is over, we have nothing to do with one another."

"Oh, but we *do*. And I can prove it."

"How?" she asked defiantly; despite her bold words she took a step backward, afraid of the proof. He pulled her swiftly, with an uncanny feel for her balance, and caught her against his chest. She had twisted defensively, trying to get her legs under her again, with the result that she ended up against him, not standing at all. The toes of one foot barely touched the ground and the other leg lay useless against his thigh. She was held up by the pressure of his arms against the small of her back. As she panted in fury one of his arms dropped beneath her buttocks and lifted her higher, crushing her hips to his belly, her breasts into his chest. She gave a little cry of frustration, which was cut short when his own mouth captured hers. His teeth bit into her lips and she found herself opening them to that sweet pain. She wanted to drink him like honey, to bring the intoxicating wine of his spirit deeper—down into her lonely body, her soul. When she felt herself slip she threw her arms around his neck and hung on with a ferocity that made him drag her even closer. His tongue washed the hunger of her mouth with spice and fire; her skin flamed where they touched; her leg curled over his with desperate strength. But she slid again. No matter what she did, she felt herself slipping from their burning contact—he was *letting* her go. When at last her legs bore her weight upon the ground, he held her pinned against him and looked down into her hot, bewildered eyes.

"Go ahead," she gasped raggedly. "Wasn't that what you wanted?"

"No—I wanted so much more. . . ."

She had never known herself capable of such rashness. She only knew what she was going to say as the words left her mouth, but she couldn't have stopped them. "Who will miss us? If you're here, everyone else must be gone." She leaned forward to bury her face in his neck.

He looked as shocked as she knew she would have in his position. She felt her head pulled back by his hand on her braid until she was forced to meet his eyes. "Why do you deliberately misunderstand me?"

he demanded gruffly. "Do you think I can just take you here in the bushes and blithely send you home in a cab, never to be bothered with you again?"

"Don't you always get what you go after?" Andrew's own words emerged from her bitterness. "You haven't gotten to where you are by being a bleeding heart."

Jess thrust her angrily away from him, though he still gripped her arms with a strength that brought tears to her eyes. "You think I'm a monster, don't you? Not a man, with a man's needs and hopes. Well, I'll admit to being selfish, so selfish that I wanted all of you, Kate—your beauty, your passion, your faith. And add another fault—pride. I'm too proud to take less than that."

He stepped back, releasing her with a wrench that jarred him as much as it did her. He pressed the heels of his hands into his brow, but it didn't hide the pain in his face or voice. "Why do you think so badly of me?"

"It's happened to me before. Andrew . . ."

"Andrew! I'm sick to death of standing next to Andrew Keene in your eyes. What do I have in common with *him*?"

"It's your whole being, Jess. You're ambitious, driven, calculating, shrewd—you'd rather die than let a human weakness come between you and what you see as a professional obligation—all those things are what make you and Andrew successful businessmen."

"You haven't named one characteristic that you don't share with me. Nor one that you could call bad and mean it. You're being awfully obtuse. If you set such store by reason, *use* it, Kate—for both our sakes."

She glared at him uneasily, warned against opening her mouth by the suspicion that he spoke truth. Andrew had never appealed to her reason. He had never appealed to her senses in quite the same volatile way that Jess did—merely to her blind, romantic notions about building a life's partnership with an admirable man. She had been quite willing to think Andrew was that man because he had all the surface features. Yet here stood an admirable man, so honest and giving that he had presented her with chance after chance to correct her mistake . . .

Jess continued in a soft voice, "We're two of a kind, Kate, and Andrew Keene has nothing to do with us. If I judged all women by Genevieve, I never would have . . ." He stopped abruptly and looked away.

Her eyes flared. "Why, you did, didn't you! You thought I was the same kind of cold, faithless . . ." She shut up, realizing that the subject of her harsh words was a woman he had loved.

But Jess picked up her sentence, ". . . shallow, unreachable, yes. I was afraid . . . the hurt is hard to get over, isn't it?"

They suffered a self-conscious moment of silence; then Kate admitted quietly, "I guess I didn't give you much evidence that I was different."

His slow smile cheered her, then brought out a flush. "Oh, you gave me a bit—every time you kissed me you made it quite clear that you wanted me as much as I wanted you."

"Arrogant!" she accused, pretending indignation and turning away to give herself time to think. She heard leaves crunch, felt his breath on her ear, then his lips on her neck. The heat that flared through her proved all his words.

"I'll admit to shrewd," he murmured.

"Will you, now!"

"I believe you did call me shrewd."

"I also called you ambitious and calculating."

"You have inspired my highest ambition, Kate," he vowed, gently turning her to face him. "To make you my wife."

Her eyes dipped away from his, suddenly shy, and she replied with a touch of her old bantering humor, "It's a good thing I like ambitious men."

His hands slipped up her sides, leaving her flesh molten, and came up to tenderly cup the sides of her face. "Then you *will* marry me?"

"I also called you calculating—it probably comes as no surprise to you that the sun is going down and the temperature is dropping. I have no desire to freeze to death out here arguing with you. I'd rather say yes and go inside and get warm."

"Don't be flip. Kiss me."

"We're going to end up in the bushes."

"No, we're not." And he picked her up bodily. "Everyone *is* gone by now, you know. Joel and Audrey are locked in the darkroom with twenty-five rolls of undeveloped film, and the house is empty. We're only four hundred feet from the lawn—think we can make it?"

"I can if you can."

"It's a dare then, is it? Humph!" He started forward. She giggled softly and nestled her cheek against his strong, proud heartbeat. "I like the feel of you in my arms," he said. "But this is even better than last night."

"What?"

"Oh, yes, who do you think put you to bed?"

"You devil!"

"No, last night I was an angel. You tried to keep me with you, but I valiantly resisted."

"Well, there'll be no more of that," she decreed.

"No."

She nestled closer, pleased that the lights of the house were now so close. "I kissed you, did I? In my sleep?"

"You did."

"Boy, have I got some dreams to tell you about!"

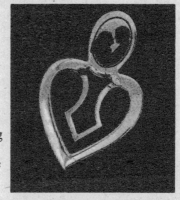

IT'S YOUR OWN SPECIAL TIME
Contemporary romances for today's women.
Each month, six very special love stories will be yours
from SILHOUETTE.

$1.75 each

☐ 104 Vitek	☐ 131 Stanford	☐ 159 Tracy	☐ 186 Howard
☐ 105 Eden	☐ 132 Wisdom	☐ 160 Hampson	☐ 187 Scott
☐ 106 Dailey	☐ 133 Rowe	☐ 161 Trent	☐ 188 Cork
☐ 107 Bright	☐ 134 Charles	☐ 162 Ashby	☐ 189 Stephens
☐ 108 Hampson	☐ 135 Logan	☐ 163 Roberts	☐ 190 Hampson
☐ 109 Vernon	☐ 136 Hampson	☐ 164 Browning	☐ 191 Browning
☐ 110 Trent	☐ 137 Hunter	☐ 165 Young	☐ 192 John
☐ 111 South	☐ 138 Wilson	☐ 166 Wisdom	☐ 193 Trent
☐ 112 Stanford	☐ 139 Vitek	☐ 167 Hunter	☐ 194 Barry
☐ 113 Browning	☐ 140 Erskine	☐ 168 Carr	☐ 195 Dailey
☐ 114 Michaels	☐ 142 Browning	☐ 169 Scott	☐ 196 Hampson
☐ 115 John	☐ 143 Roberts	☐ 170 Ripy	☐ 197 Summers
☐ 116 Lindley	☐ 144 Goforth	☐ 171 Hill	☐ 198 Hunter
☐ 117 Scott	☐ 145 Hope	☐ 172 Browning	☐ 199 Roberts
☐ 118 Dailey	☐ 146 Michaels	☐ 173 Camp	☐ 200 Lloyd
☐ 119 Hampson	☐ 147 Hampson	☐ 174 Sinclair	☐ 201 Starr
☐ 120 Carroll	☐ 148 Cork	☐ 175 Jarrett	☐ 202 Hampson
☐ 121 Langan	☐ 149 Saunders	☐ 176 Vitek	☐ 203 Browning
☐ 122 Scofield	☐ 150 Major	☐ 177 Dailey	☐ 204 Carroll
☐ 123 Sinclair	☐ 151 Hampson	☐ 178 Hampson	☐ 205 Maxam
☐ 124 Beckman	☐ 152 Halston	☐ 179 Beckman	☐ 206 Manning
☐ 125 Bright	☐ 153 Dailey	☐ 180 Roberts	☐ 207 Windham
☐ 126 St. George	☐ 154 Beckman	☐ 181 Terrill	☐ 208 Halston
☐ 127 Roberts	☐ 155 Hampson	☐ 182 Clay	☐ 209 LaDame
☐ 128 Hampson	☐ 156 Sawyer	☐ 183 Stanley	☐ 210 Eden
☐ 129 Converse	☐ 157 Vitek	☐ 184 Hardy	☐ 211 Walters
☐ 130 Hardy	☐ 158 Reynolds	☐ 185 Hampson	☐ 212 Young

$1.95 each

☐ 213 Dailey	☐ 219 Cork	☐ 225 St. George	☐ 231 Dailey
☐ 214 Hampson	☐ 220 Hampson	☐ 226 Hampson	☐ 232 Hampson
☐ 215 Roberts	☐ 221 Browning	☐ 227 Beckman	☐ 233 Vernon
☐ 216 Saunders	☐ 222 Carroll	☐ 228 King	☐ 234 Smith
☐ 217 Vitek	☐ 223 Summers	☐ 229 Thornton	☐ 235 James
☐ 218 Hunter	☐ 224 Langan	☐ 230 Stevens	☐ 236 Maxam

Silhouette Romance

$1.95 each

☐ 237 Wilson	☐ 263 Wilson	☐ 289 Saunders	☐ 315 Smith
☐ 238 Cork	☐ 264 Vine	☐ 290 Hunter	☐ 316 Macomber
☐ 239 McKay	☐ 265 Adams	☐ 291 McKay	☐ 317 Langan
☐ 240 Hunter	☐ 266 Trent	☐ 292 Browning	☐ 318 Herrington
☐ 241 Wisdom	☐ 267 Chase	☐ 293 Morgan	☐ 319 Lloyd
☐ 242 Brooke	☐ 268 Hunter	☐ 294 Cockcroft	☐ 320 Brooke
☐ 243 Saunders	☐ 269 Smith	☐ 295 Vernon	☐ 321 Glenn
☐ 244 Sinclair	☐ 270 Camp	☐ 296 Paige	☐ 322 Hunter
☐ 245 Trent	☐ 271 Allison	☐ 297 Young	☐ 323 Browning
☐ 246 Carroll	☐ 272 Forrest	☐ 298 Hunter	☐ 324 Maxam
☐ 247 Halldorson	☐ 273 Beckman	☐ 299 Roberts	☐ 325 Smith
☐ 248 St. George	☐ 274 Roberts	☐ 300 Stephens	☐ 326 Lovan
☐ 249 Scofield	☐ 275 Browning	☐ 301 Palmer	☐ 327 James
☐ 250 Hampson	☐ 276 Vernon	☐ 302 Smith	☐ 328 Palmer
☐ 251 Wilson	☐ 277 Wilson	☐ 303 Langan	☐ 329 Broadrick
☐ 252 Roberts	☐ 278 Hunter	☐ 304 Cork	☐ 330 Ferrell
☐ 253 James	☐ 279 Ashby	☐ 305 Browning	☐ 331 Michaels
☐ 254 Palmer	☐ 280 Roberts	☐ 306 Gordon	☐ 332 McCarty
☐ 255 Smith	☐ 281 Lovan	☐ 307 Wildman	☐ 333 Page
☐ 256 Hampson	☐ 282 Halldorson	☐ 308 Young	☐ 334 Hohl
☐ 257 Hunter	☐ 283 Payne	☐ 309 Hardy	☐ 335 Bishop
☐ 258 Ashby	☐ 284 Young	☐ 310 Hunter	☐ 336 Young
☐ 259 English	☐ 285 Gray	☐ 311 Gray	☐ 337 Sands
☐ 260 Martin	☐ 286 Cork	☐ 312 Vernon	☐ 338 Gray
☐ 261 Saunders	☐ 287 Joyce	☐ 313 Rainville	☐ 339 Morland
☐ 262 John	☐ 288 Smith	☐ 314 Palmer	

SILHOUETTE BOOKS, Department SB/1

1230 Avenue of the Americas
New York, NY 10020

Please send me the books I have checked above. I am enclosing $_____
(please add 75¢ to cover postage and handling. NYS and NYC residents please
add appropriate sales tax). Send check or money order—no cash or C.O.D.'s
please. Allow six weeks for delivery.

NAME _____

ADDRESS _____

CITY _____ STATE/ZIP _____

Silhouette Romance